RUNNING ON EMPTY

SONYA SPREEN BATES

WITHDRAWN

ORCA BOOK PUBLISHERS

Library and Archives Canada Cataloguing in Publication

Bates, Sonya Spreen, author
Running on empty / Sonya Spreen Bates.
(Orca sports)

Issued in print and electronic formats.
ISBN 978-1-4598-1653-4 (softcover).—ISBN 978-1-4598-1654-1 (pdf).—
ISBN 978-1-4598-1655-8 (epub)

I. Title. II. Series: Orca sports
PS8603.A8486R86 2018   jc813'.6   c2017-904494-x   c2017-904495-8

First published in the United States, 2018
Library of Congress Control Number: 2017911446

Summary: In this high-interest sports novel for teens, Leon is
devastated after an injury gets him bumped off the relay team.

*Orca Book Publishers is dedicated to preserving the environment and has printed
this book on Forest Stewardship Council® certified paper.*

Orca Book Publishers gratefully acknowledges the support for its publishing
programs provided by the following agencies: the Government of Canada
through the Canada Book Fund and the Canada Council for the Arts,
and the Province of British Columbia through the BC Arts Council
and the Book Publishing Tax Credit.

Edited by Tanya Trafford
Cover photography by iStock.com/martin-dm
Author photo by Megan Bates

ORCA BOOK PUBLISHERS
www.orcabook.com

Printed and bound in Canada.

21 20 19 18 • 4 3 2 1

If you fall behind, run faster. Never give up, never surrender, and rise up against the odds.

—Jesse Jackson

Chapter One

I never thought I'd get a chance to make history. And yet here I was, one race away from sending my school into the record books.

It was May of my junior year. Gilburn High had made the interschool track championships. Nothing new there. We'd taken home the trophy six years running. But this year was different. Rivalry between the schools in Monterey was fierce. If we won again, we would have the longest winning streak in fifty years. The thing is, McKenzie

High was strong. With a few talented freshmen and sophomores coming through the ranks, they'd already won two golds, four silvers and a bunch of minor placings. All that was left to run was the open boys 4x100m relay. We were neck and neck in the points tally. It was the deciding race.

That's where I came in. Coach Dunstan had chosen me as anchor. Me. Leon Kline. A junior.

All I had to do was grab the baton from Riley Manson and take it across the finish line. First. Beat Harvey Miller from Newbury. Beat Jamar Dennison from McKenzie. Beat everyone. Otherwise McKenzie would go home with the trophy. No pressure, right?

I felt limber and energized as I lined up on the final stretch. I was in lane four, a nice position in the middle of the track. Harvey Miller was on my right in lane five, Jamar Dennison in lane six. With any luck, Riley would come around the bend in first place, and all I'd need to do was hold the lead.

The starter called, "On your marks," and the first runners stepped up to the blocks. Hunter Wallace was starting for us. He's our fastest out of the blocks, but he's been known to make false starts, so I was a little nervous.

"Get set."

The gun sounded and they were off. Hunter kept his cool and didn't jump the gun. McKenzie's starter got out first though. He bolted out of the blocks, a half stride down the track before anyone else even moved. What surprised me was the kid waiting for him at the first exchange. It was the squirt who'd come second in the open 200. At about four foot nothing and eighty pounds tops, he was easily the smallest kid on the track. But boy, could he run. He took the baton cleanly from the McKenzie starter and shot down the straight like an arrow.

Adrenaline started pumping as the runners raced into the second exchange, McKenzie's runner in the lead, followed closely by Sam Delaney from our team and Newbury's not far behind. Sam hit the passing zone, and Riley took off. Too fast. Sam's a great sprinter, but he'd gone all out. He couldn't catch Riley at full acceleration. Riley looked back, slowed and grabbed the baton. It had taken precious milliseconds. Milliseconds we didn't have to spare.

I crouched in position, eyes on Riley as he came around the bend. We couldn't afford to blow another change-over. He hit the exchange zone neck and neck with McKenzie and Newbury and shouted, "Go!" I took off. Eyes ahead, I ran down the track, hand stretched out behind me. I felt the reassuring thump of the baton in my palm, closed my fist over it and raced for the finish.

Both Jamar and Harvey were ahead of me. Not by much, but in 100m it doesn't take much of a lead to win. I increased my stride, arms pumping, legs and lungs burning. The gap started to close. I pushed harder. I was half a stride behind Harvey when he stumbled. I tried to jump out of the way, but it all happened so fast.

One second I was blasting down the straight, and the next I was one half of a tumbleweed spinning out of control. It was all arms and legs and hair and batons, and then we slammed into the ground.

Harvey landed on top of me, and I heard a distinct *crack*. Suddenly my leg was on fire. I gasped, tried to draw breath, wheezing for air.

Harvey rolled off me.

I curled up around my pain, trying to breathe. The stadium was quiet. Somewhere in the distance I heard a voice saying, "Medic! Get the medic!"

Then Coach Dunstan was beside me. "Don't try to move, Leon. We're getting the stretcher."

I couldn't have moved if I tried. My world was pain. Leg, lungs, head. Movement was unthinkable. I lay looking at the sky, waiting to be carried away from what should have been my moment of triumph.

"I'm so sorry," said Harvey.

Chapter Two

Everyone was really nice after the accident. All the guys came to visit me in the hospital, laughed about the spectacular wipeout I'd had. Broken leg, cracked rib, concussion. It was pretty impressive for a running accident. Then the excitement died down, the surgery was over, and I was left lying on the couch with my leg propped up, watching TV. Now, lying on the couch all day watching TV may sound like heaven, but let me tell you, after a week I was bored to the point of madness.

The weeks passed and summer arrived. A summer of doing nothing. No beach, no swimming, no running, no biking, no skateboarding, no driving, no part-time job. A summer of hobbling around on crutches, going to physio sessions and "liking" all the photos on social media of my friends doing exactly what I wished I was doing.

My mom took to baking, like she always does in a crisis. She baked cakes and brownies and cookies and left them out for me every day before she went to work. And I ate them. Hey, I was bored—what else was there to do while I rewatched the fifth season of *Doctor Who*?

It was mid-August when she got the call from New York. That's where my grandparents live. I could hear my parents talking from my room. Not fighting, but serious, emotional. My mom gets this weird crack in her voice when she's worried, so I knew something was up. Then my name was mentioned. Several times. Finally I got up and eased the door open so I could hear what they were actually saying.

"Go," said Dad. "Just go. We'll cope."
I could hear he was getting frustrated.

"I can't leave Leon now," said Mom.
"He's still doing physio, and besides, he's
just about to start his senior year."

"He's seventeen. He doesn't need his
hand held."

"But how will he get to his appoint-
ments? To school?"

"He'll take the bus," said Dad.

"But his leg—"

"It'll do him good," said Dad. "He's
been lazing around here all summer doing
nothing but getting fat. It's about time he
got off his butt and did something to help
himself."

The words stung. I'd seen the looks Dad
gave me when he got home from work but
he'd never said anything. Not a word.

"David. That's a bit harsh," said Mom.

"It's the truth, Mira. You can't bubble-
wrap him forever. What's he gonna do
when he finishes school? Are you going
to hold his hand while he looks for a job?
Drive him to McDonald's to sling burgers?

Because he can kiss college goodbye. No one's going to give him an athletic scholarship with that leg."

"Shush," said Mom. "He'll hear you."

"Well, he's got to face reality at some point," said Dad, but he did lower his voice. "Look, if anything happened to your parents and you didn't go out there, you'd never forgive yourself."

That was enough for me. I shuffled down the hall and into the living room.

"What's going on?" I said, avoiding looking at Dad.

Mom and Dad exchanged glances.

"Has something happened?"

"Grandma fell going down the stairs into the subway," said Mom. "She broke her hip. She's stable, but her recovery is going to take some time. There's no one to look out for your grandfather. You know his memory isn't quite what it used to be anymore."

That was an understatement. Last time we went out to visit, he turned the tap on in the bathtub and then totally forgot about it. We didn't know until Mom saw the water running down the hallway.

"So you're going out to New York?" I asked.

Mom hesitated. "I don't know. I hate to leave you..."

"Mom, I'm not an invalid," I said, then looked at Dad. "I can take care of myself."

"But it's senior year...and I don't know how long I will be gone."

"So? Just go, Mom. Seriously, I don't need you here."

She looked a bit hurt but relieved as well. "If you're sure."

"I'm sure," I said.

So Mom left for New York two days later, and that left Dad and me on our own. By the time September came around, I was almost looking forward to school starting.

Chapter Three

It was at my last physio session before school started that I met Casey De Vries. Best thing that had happened all summer. Or so I thought. Dad dropped me off on his way to the fire station, so I was hanging around looking at year-old copies of *Sports Illustrated*. This girl came out of one of the treatment rooms and dropped into a chair opposite me. She was by far the best-looking girl I'd ever seen. Short hair, a turned-up nose and huge eyes that were a little too bright, almost teary.

Her right arm was wrapped in a pressure bandage.

"Man, I swear they enjoy it," she said, leaning her head back and closing her eyes.

There was no one else around, so I assumed she was talking to me. "Enjoy what?" I asked, putting down the magazine.

Her ice-blue eyes opened, and her gaze locked on mine. Almost a challenge. "Inflicting pain. What else?"

"Huh. You got that right," I said, looking away. Just thinking about what was coming made my leg ache.

"Like, what kind of person would choose physiotherapy as a career? Knowing how much it hurts?"

I laughed. "Maybe they were medieval torturers in a previous life."

She smiled, and I was glad I could make her smile.

"What's wrong with you?" she said.

I shrugged. "Broke my leg."

"And you come to the torture chamber for that?"

I looked up to see if she was laughing at me. She was.

"It was a bad break," I said, crossing my arms across my chest. "Why, what's your big claim to fame?"

"Burn," she said, holding up her bandaged arm. "Second degree, all the way up to my neck."

I cringed. "Hell, that must've hurt."

"It did," she said. "Still does."

I didn't know what else to say, so I said nothing.

"Hey, don't let it get you down," she said. "Life goes on."

"'Course it does," I said.

There was an awkward silence, but when I glanced over at her, she was smirking at me.

"What school do you go to?" she said.

"Gilburn," I said. "Senior year."

"Lucky you," she said. "I've got two more years." Her eyes went wide. "Wait. Did you say Gilburn?"

"Yeah."

"I knew I'd seen you before." She pointed a finger at me using her good arm, the one without the bandage. "You're that kid, aren't you? The one Harvey Miller took out at the athletics meet."

I stared at her. "You go to Newbury?"

"Yeah. Harvey Miller's in my homeroom."

"Small world." I looked away and then back again. "What do you mean, you've seen me before?"

"On YouTube. Surely you've seen the video?"

I shook my head. She dug out her phone, then came over and sat in the chair next to me while she pulled up the site. Her right side was toward me now, and I could see the angry red scar spreading out of the bandage and up her neck.

"It's hilarious. I mean, I'm sure it wasn't at the time. But just watch it. You will laugh."

She hit *Play* and I leaned in so I could see the screen. She was watching too, head down, a slight smile on her lips. I could smell her perfume. Something musky and dark.

I moved back slightly and forced myself to concentrate on the video.

Someone had been filming from the front of the grandstand, right near the finish line. They zoomed in on Harvey Miller. There I was next to him, and Jamar Dennison on his other side, all of us looking back at the runners barreling around the bend. We took off within milliseconds of each other. The camera was still on Harvey, but I could see my face clearly two steps behind him, teeth bared, grimacing like I was in pain. I'd never seen a video of myself running before, and I was a bit embarrassed by the weird face I was pulling.

We were maybe twenty meters from the finish line when Harvey stumbled sideways. His face took on a look of surprise I'd only seen in comedy shows, mouth open in an O, eyes stretched wide. Then it was my turn. And the girl was right—the change in expression would have been hilarious if I hadn't known what came next. Harvey came down on me, shoulder slamming into my body. I looked away. I didn't need to see the rest. I remembered it all too well.

"Maybe it's not so funny," she said, shutting off the phone.

"Leon Kline?"

I looked up. It was a new guy, big, with a shaved head.

"Oooh. Bad luck," she said, grimacing. "That one doesn't have an ounce of sympathy."

"Great. Just what I need." I got up and started toward the treatment rooms, trying as hard as I could not to limp. I don't know why it seemed to matter whether she saw me limp.

"Hey, Gilburn," she called after me.

I turned back.

"Just remember, pain is temporary."

I could hear her laughter following me all the way down the corridor.

Chapter Four

Labor Day weekend passed in a flash, and then it was back to school. I'd known the first day would be tough. Despite all the physio I'd had, I still had a bit of a limp, and my endurance was pitiful. I hadn't known how tough it would be though. How everything I looked at, everyone I spoke to, would remind me that I wasn't Leon Kline sprinter and long jumper anymore.

It began as soon as I arrived at school, before I'd even stepped foot inside the building. Because first there were the steps to deal with. There were twenty of them, climbing steeply up to the front of the school. No big deal until today. Maybe it wouldn't have mattered so much if Dad had dropped me off, but he'd been called out to a fire in the middle of the night, and I'd had to walk. They looked like Mount Everest.

I was sweating by the time I got to the top. I hobbled through the door and stopped to rest in front of the trophy cabinet. The Athletics Championship Cup was gone, of course, and the cabinet looked empty without it.

"Don't beat yourself up about it," said Coach Dunstan, coming up behind me. "We'll get it back this year."

"Yeah, of course we will," I said, trying to smile.

"It wasn't your fault. It was an accident." He put his hand on my shoulder, playing the concerned-uncle routine. "It could have happened to anyone."

"Yeah. I know."

He walked off, and I ambled down the hall toward my locker. It could have happened to anyone. Sure. But it hadn't happened to anyone. It had happened to me. It was me everyone was staring at, me they were whispering about behind their hands.

"Hey, Kline. Missed you at the beach this summer," said Tyler West, shoving his bag into his locker, three down from mine. He looked tanned, his long blond hair bleached by the sun. "Where were you?"

"I was kind of busy," I said, not looking at him. I spun the dial on my lock, then gave it a slam with my fist when it didn't open.

"You missed out, man. The surf was great," he said.

I didn't say anything. Just kept fiddling with the lock.

"You should have come down last weekend. The waves were awesome. I caught a ten-footer and rode it all the way home." He struck a surfing pose, grinning like a baboon.

I slammed the locker again and turned to face him. "Really? Well, I'm not doing much surfing at the moment, but thanks anyway."

He looked down at my leg, then away. "Oh yeah. I guess not." He closed his locker. "Catch you later?" he said, already loping down the hall.

"Whatever," I muttered.

I finally got my locker open and stowed my bag. This wasn't the way things were supposed to be. This was my senior year. I was meant to be captain of the athletics team, getting my gold letter and enjoying life at the top. But here I was, sweating like I'd done a full workout, just from climbing the stairs.

"Leon!"

I looked up to see Sam sauntering toward me.

"You look like your dog died," he said, giving me a clap on the back that sent me reeling.

"Nah, nothing like that," I said. I banged the locker door shut, and we headed for homeroom. Sam slowed his steps so I wouldn't get left behind.

"You watch that movie I lent you?" he said.

I hadn't, but I didn't let on.

"Yeah, sure. I really liked it," I said.

"Liar." He punched me in the shoulder.

I staggered sideways, and he grabbed my arm so I didn't run into a kid coming the other way.

"Look out," he said to the freshman, like it was his fault. Then, quieter, to me: "Sorry, Leon. Didn't mean to knock you over."

I shrugged his hand off. "You didn't. It doesn't matter."

"You started running yet?" he said, looking down at my leg.

I stood up straighter and made an effort not to limp. "Not yet. I've got a doctor's appointment after school. Hopefully he'll give me the green light."

"Just in time for tryouts," said Sam. He smiled, like this should cheer me up.

"Yeah, wouldn't that be great," I said. I knew better though. Even if the doctor did give me the go-ahead to start running, I was nowhere near fit enough to make the team. It would be a long time before I ran a sprint race again.

We went into the classroom, and I slid into a seat and pulled out my phone. I could hear the conversations going on around me, everyone talking about their summer, the places they'd gone, the things they'd done. I kept my eyes down, focused on the screen, like there was something on it I couldn't drag myself away from.

Chapter Five

It was six o'clock before I got home. Dad was still out, and Nan and Pop were there, making dinner. The smell of sausages frying hit me as soon as I walked in the door. I could hear the sound of the news coming from the TV in the kitchen.

"Leon, come and say hello to your grand-parents," Nan called out as I tried to sneak by without them hearing me.

I poked my head in the door, hoping to just give a wave and move on, but Nan tottered over to me, arms outstretched.

"Look at you, Leon. First day of senior year," she said, standing back, clutching my elbows with a grip that would rival a boa constrictor's. "You've grown so tall."

I grinned stupidly, not knowing quite what to say, until she released her death grip.

"How's the leg?" asked Pop.

I shrugged. "Coming along. I get the pin out next month."

He nodded. "Nasty accident, that. Where was that boy from? The one who tripped you up?"

"Newbury."

"Hmmph. You'd think a boy from Newbury would know to stay in his lane."

"It wasn't his fault, Pop. It was an accident." We'd had this conversation before. Pop was a cop until he retired, and he's the most suspicious person I know. I peered into the pan of greasy sausages. The smell was making me drool. "Dad's not back yet?"

"Won't be back for a while," said Pop. "After the heat we've had this summer, that fire would have taken off like a tornado. It'll take a while to put it out. Wait, here's something about it on the news." He turned the sound up, and we all crowded in to watch.

"Monterey firefighters have had a busy Labor Day weekend," said the presenter, a middle-aged blond lady in a teal-green suit. "They were called out in the early hours of the morning after lightning struck a tree at Mulligan's Creek. The blaze has now been contained. A second fire was reported only hours later in a warehouse in Port Fernandez. The cause has yet to be determined. Arson has not been ruled out. Damage is estimated at $500,000."

Pop leaned back and gestured at the TV. "Can you believe that? Like there wasn't enough trouble in the world, we have thugs setting fires and putting people like your father in danger. That's the fifth one this summer. There are lives at stake here—don't they know that?"

He didn't seem to expect an answer, and I didn't give him one. I'd heard it all before. Pretty soon he'd be asking me if I was going

Sonya Spreen Bates

to join the force. Become a firefighter or a cop, like my father, like him. Right now I didn't want to go there.

"I've got homework," I said.

In my room I threw my bag on the bed and turned on the computer. I found the next episode of *The Simpsons* and clicked *Play*.

I hadn't been entirely truthful with Pop about my leg. Yeah, the doctor had said I'd get the pin out next month. Yeah, he'd even said I could start running again if I wanted. It was something else he had said that I hadn't told them.

I settled back, trying to keep my mind off it. I just wanted to forget it had ever happened. So far, I'd failed miserably.

I was five minutes into the show, still struggling to concentrate, when I heard a *ding*. Someone had messaged me. I clicked on the icon.

Hey, Gilburn. Remember me? Your fellow torture victim. The name's Casey, in case you were wondering!

Did I remember her? Of course I did. In fact, I'd thought about her all weekend, although I'd never tell her that.

> **Hi, Casey. Physio, Friday afternoon, right? How did you find me?**

> > *That big bald guy called your name when he took you into the torture chamber, remember? I have a memory like an elephant.*

> **LOL. Wish I did. Must come in handy during exam time.**

> > *It's a selective memory. Hahaha. How was the first day?*

Suddenly I wasn't laughing anymore. What a question. Truthfully? It had been one of the worst days of my life. The real question was, should I tell her the truth?

I must have taken too long to answer, because she messaged again before I could think of what to say.

> > *That bad, huh?*

> > **Pretty much. You?**

> > *Same. At least everyone wasn't staring at you.*

27

Yeah, they were.

Why? So you broke your leg. What's the big deal? It'll heal, right? And you'll go back to being normal again.

That's the thing. I wasn't going to be normal again. Not like I was before. That's what I'd learned today at the doctor's appointment. He'd said I'd healed, and healed well, but I'd never be just like I was before the accident.

Leon?

Yeah, I'm here.

Your leg will be okay, right?

Sort of. The thing is, it's a bit short.

What do you mean, a bit short?

Shorter than the other one.

Bummer.

Yeah. Sucks to be me, eh?

I don't know. Burn scars vs short leg. I think I'd take the leg.

I could have kicked myself. Kicked myself with my stupid runty short leg. I'd completely forgotten about her burns, completely forgotten why she'd been at the physio in the first place.

You've got me on that one. Sorry.
No worries. Nice to know someone
can talk to me without thinking about
me as a burn victim.
Make you a deal. I'll treat you like a
normal person if you do the same for me.
You got it.

The door to my bedroom opened, and Pop came in. I flipped my laptop shut.

"Homework, is it?" he said, narrowing his eyes.

I shrugged. "Just talking to a friend."

He stared at me for a minute but in the end just said, "Dinner's ready."

"Thanks. I'll be there in a sec."

He eyed me for a moment longer, then left, leaving the door open.

I opened the laptop again, but Casey had already logged off.

Chapter Six

Athletics training started a week later.

Coach tried to talk me into going, told me I could start out slow and see how far I got before tryouts. Maybe try a different event that didn't put so much strain on my leg, like shot put or hammer throw. I wasn't convinced. I was a sprinter. Always had been. It was who I was.

Don't get me wrong. I did try. I got up really early one morning, while it was still dark, put on my gear and headed out. I knew I wouldn't be able to run far, or fast, but I wasn't prepared for just how slow I was. My right leg, the short one, just couldn't seem to get going. It was weak, useless. I'd power through with the left leg and fall hard on the right, take a quick step and onto the left again. It felt like any moment the bone would snap again, which I knew was ridiculous, but I couldn't get the thought out of my head. I stumped along for a block, maybe two, until Stan Martin from across the road overtook me with his dog. Then I dropped back to a walk and turned for home. If I couldn't stay ahead of an old man with a beer gut the size of Santa's, what hope did I have of beating anyone in a sprint?

Dad was making coffee when I got in. He raised his eyebrows when he saw me in my running gear.

"Been for a run?" he asked.

"Yeah."

He grunted and nodded. Like it was normal. Like I hadn't spent all summer on the couch.

31

I waited for him to say more. To ask me how the run was, how my leg was. After all, he was the one who got me into running in the first place. Now he didn't even seem interested. He scooped coffee into the basket and filled the pot with water, totally ignoring me. I knew there'd been a bit of tension between us since Mom left, but I thought he'd say *something*.

"I better hit the shower," I said.

He nodded again and went back to scooping coffee. I didn't bother to tell him he'd already put in enough for two or three pots.

Sam was a little more enthusiastic. He'd been nagging me all week about trying a run, ever since the doc had given me the all clear. Now I wished I'd never told him.

"So how was it?" he said as soon as he saw me at school.

"It was fine," I said. "No big deal."

He grinned, as easy to please as a puppy. "So you're coming to training?"

"Nah, I don't think so." I grabbed my books and headed down the hallway, hoping he'd drop it.

Sam's never been one to take a hint. "Why not?" he said. "We need you on the team, Leon."

"No you don't," I said, not slowing my pace. Not that it mattered. A snail could keep up with me at full pace.

"Yes we do. You're one of our best sprinters. How will we get the trophy back without you?"

And that was the ugly truth. They probably wouldn't get the trophy back without me. Not that I was a superstar or anything, but almost half the team had graduated the previous year, and the sophomores and juniors coming up were average at best. I'd lost the trophy for Gilburn, and now I couldn't even do my bit to get it back.

"All right. You want to know the truth?" I said, stopping and turning to look at him. "I sucked. I sucked big-time. I can't run and I can't sprint. I can't even walk without looking like an old man. I'm sorry if you're disappointed, but that's the way it is, and there's nothing I can do about it. You'll have to get the trophy without me."

I stared at him for a second, then turned and stomped down the hall. I hadn't realized I'd been shouting until I noticed everyone staring at me. I put my head down and kept walking.

When the final bell rang at the end of the day, I grabbed my books and headed out without talking to anyone. I was halfway home when I thought I saw Casey De Vries. She was outside a 7-Eleven, in a group of about ten or twelve kids. I only caught a glimpse, a split-second side view, before someone moved between us and I lost sight of her. It was enough to send a rush of adrenaline through me, though, and I went a little closer, hoping to spot her again.

That's when I saw Zane Bailey. He's a kid who used to go to Gilburn. Halfway through my junior year he just disappeared. I never knew whether he dropped out or got kicked out, and I didn't really care. I was just glad he was gone.

The group went into the store, and I saw a flash of Casey's blond hair again. I suppose I could have gone in after them. That seemed a bit weird though. We'd been messaging each other a lot, but I'd only really met her once. I didn't think she'd appreciate me following her around. I decided to send her a text instead.

Hey. Just got out of school. What are you up to?

There was no reply. I walked past slowly, half hoping she might see me and come out and half dreading the same thing. After all, what would I say to her? Would she even let on that she knew me when she was with her friends? And if it was her, what was she doing hanging out with a guy like Zane Bailey?

I kept walking and nothing happened, and gradually my heartbeat slowed down to a normal rhythm. My brain wouldn't stop, though, and I thought about her all the way home.

Chapter Seven

It was a couple of days before I heard from Casey again. I was beginning to wonder if she'd seen me outside the 7-Eleven and thought I was some weird stalker or something. Turned out it wasn't her at all, because she said she'd been to see a specialist in LA and had forgotten to take her phone.

We talked almost every day after that. About stupid stuff. TV shows, movies, school, friends. We shared YouTube videos and funny quotes on Facebook, and Snapchatted goofy pictures. I didn't run into her at physio again, and we didn't talk about meeting up.

Then, around the beginning of October, out of the blue she texted.

Hey. Wanna go for a run?

My shoulders slumped. A run? I hadn't run since that time back in September when Stan Martin and his dog had left me in the dust. I hadn't gone to athletics training. I couldn't even watch athletics training. In fact, except for Sam and Riley, I'd taken to avoiding the guys on the team so I didn't have to listen to them talking about it.

I'm not really running anymore.

Why the hell not?

You know why.

That's lame. So you've got a short leg.

What's the big deal?

I can't run.

You mean you won't.

No, I can't.

That's bull. You're just chicken.

Now I was getting mad. We'd only met once. She knew nothing about what I could and couldn't do. Where did she get off calling me chicken?

Am not. I can't run. I've tried.

Chicken.

Go to hell.

Prove it.

What?

Come out on Saturday and prove to me that you can't run. Then I'll leave you alone.

I wanted to tell her to get off my back. I didn't have to prove anything. But I also wanted to see her. And if this was the only way...

Chicken.

Fine. Saturday morning. Early. I don't need anyone standing around gawking at me.

You're on.

She was waiting for me under a tree when I got to the park. She looked different than I remembered. Shorter, skinnier.

She wore running shorts and a T-shirt and a tight sleeve on her right arm. Her hair was pink. Her smile was the same, though. A grin that made you wonder what she knew about you that you didn't want her to know.

"I was beginning to think you'd chickened out," she said.

"Nah, the bus was late," I said. I'd chosen a park a bit out of town so I wouldn't run into anyone I knew. "You changed your hair."

She shrugged. "Gives people something to stare at besides my scar."

"Huh." The pink hair suited her. And it did draw attention away from her burns. I didn't know how to tell her that without it sounding weird.

"So are we going to do this or not?" she said, stretching her legs.

"Do we have to? It's stupid. I told you I can't run."

"I'll be the judge of that," she said, taking off across the grass. "Come on. Try to keep up."

She wasn't going fast, but it was too fast for me. I watched her, my chest tightening as she got farther away. I didn't want her to see me running. I could imagine what I looked like, and I knew it wasn't pretty. But she kept going and didn't look back, so after a minute I set off after her.

It was hard going. The grass was long and uneven, and I had to concentrate on not turning an ankle—either of them. I took short steps and kept my eyes on the ground ahead. I could feel myself limping, the uneven rhythm of it, the unbalanced weight. There was nothing I could do about it.

Casey reached the edge of the park and bent down to tie her shoe. The gap between us started closing, and I slowed down. Not that I'd been going any great speed in the first place. Somewhat slower than a jog and faster than a walk. But I was breathing hard already, the months on the couch catching up to me.

"You see?" I said as I neared her. "I can't—"

I'm sure she heard me. She was only a few steps away. But she stood up and started running again. Out the gate and down the road.

"Casey!" I said, slowing to a walk. "Come back. I can't—"

"Yes you can," she yelled over her shoulder. "You already have." She kept running.

I stopped and threw my hands up in frustration, watching her getting smaller as she continued on down the street. Then she waved with her bandaged arm and turned a corner, disappearing from view.

She wasn't coming back. I knew it for certain. She was going for her run, and I had a choice—follow her or go home, tail tucked between my legs. I looked back across the park to where we'd started. It was a good two hundred meters. And she was right. I had run it. No, not like I would have six months ago. It had been slow, painful, but definitely a run. Or at least a jog.

I looked back at the corner where she'd disappeared. There was no one on the street. No one to see me. No one to look and point. Not even Casey. I pulled off my hoodie, slung it over my shoulders and hit the pavement.

Chapter Eight

The house was dead quiet when I got home, like it often was these days. I kinda liked it. With Dad at work and Mom in New York, I could do my own thing. No one asked me where I was going, what I was doing or when I would be back.

Not that I didn't talk to Mom. We messaged and talked on Skype. I told her about my not going to tryouts but that I still wanted to start running again. She got that funny crack in her voice when I told her that. And here's the thing. If she'd been home, I probably would have let her talk me out of it. Got back on the couch and eaten another brownie. Only she wasn't there, and Casey was, and Casey wasn't going to let me take the easy way out.

I didn't tell Mom about Casey. I hadn't told anyone about Casey. There was something mysterious about her, almost dangerous. She was like a delicious secret, too good to be shared. Mom might worry. Maybe she'd get so worried she'd come home. That was the last thing I wanted.

If she had been here, she probably would have figured it out—I'm not a good liar. And if Dad had had an ounce of parental radar, he would have too. As it was, he did his thing and I did mine. I didn't tell him about Casey. I didn't tell him about the D I got on my last history test. And I didn't tell him I'd been running. I knew what he thought of me. I'd heard him loud and clear the night Mom got the call from New York. I owed him nothing.

Casey and I now ran most Saturday mornings. Or rather, Casey ran and I limped along behind her, trying to keep her in sight. My running was improving. I wasn't quite as pathetic as I was that first day, but I was still slow. Painfully slow.

After the run we'd sit in the grass and talk. At least, I talked. I told her everything. About Sam and Riley and the other guys at school and how I almost never saw them anymore. About Coach Dunstan avoiding me and me avoiding Coach Dunstan. About my mom going to New York and me living with my dad. About the accident. About my sliding grades. Sometimes I talked so much I felt like Forrest Gump.

Casey told me absolutely nothing. Nothing important anyway. I knew she lived with her mom and her stepdad and her little half brother, Oscar, who was five. I knew she was a junior at Newbury. And that was it. She told me nothing about her friends or school or home life. And absolutely nothing about what had happened when she burned her arm. I did hint at it once when we were talking about my accident, but she quickly changed the subject. I didn't ask again.

I was curious though. Not just about her arm but about her. What kind of music she liked, what kind of food she ate, who her friends were, whether she had any pets. What she did when she wasn't out running with me. If she played sports, read books, went to the movies. I don't know how she did it, but we talked and talked and I still knew nothing when I wanted to know everything.

So one day I followed her. I know I shouldn't have, but I couldn't help myself. The feeling had been growing in me for weeks. The feeling that she was keeping secrets from me. And I needed to know.

It was a cold day in December. We'd finished our run, and as soon as we stopped moving, the sweat started chilling on our skin. Within minutes Casey was shivering, and we decided to call it a day. She headed out of the park and I'd started toward my bus stop when suddenly I just turned around. I don't recall making a conscious decision about it. It just happened.

She was going pretty quickly, and I didn't blame her. There was a chill in the wind that was rarely felt in Monterey. It made it hard to keep up, though, and I found myself breaking into a jog several times just to keep her in sight. She walked all the way down Oak, then turned up Mathers and into the industrial district. I couldn't imagine what she was doing there. It was all junkyards and storage barns and metal workshops.

She kept going, past a mechanic's, the recycle depot and a body shop, until she reached an abandoned warehouse. It looked like it had been empty for years, an old wooden structure with peeling paint, broken windowpanes and trash littering the yard. There she stopped, had a quick look around and then slipped through a sliding door into the building's dark interior.

I didn't follow her in. She would've known I'd been trailing her and would probably never speak to me again. So I sat there, sheltered from the wind by a dumpster, for half an hour. She didn't come out, and neither did anyone else. I didn't get it. Was she living there? She didn't look or act like a homeless kid. She had nice clothes, a cell phone, money to color her hair. And she went to Newbury with Harvey Miller. Or at least she said she did.

So what was going on?

I sat there, thoughts running circles in my mind, until my butt started getting numb. Then I got up and headed for the bus, as clueless about her as I'd been before but ten times more curious.

Chapter Nine

Christmas holidays were approaching. I found myself wishing they were over before they had even begun. Not because I loved school or anything. But because Mom had bought me a ticket to New York. I was spending the holidays on Grandma and Grandpa's couch and that meant almost a month without seeing Casey. That may not seem like a big deal when I was getting Christmas in the Big Apple, but I was getting seriously addicted. I thought about her all the time. She was exciting, stimulating, an adrenaline rush. A rush like I used to get busting through the finish line at the front of the pack.

On Wednesday of the last week of school I was sitting in the lunchroom with Sam and Riley when I got a message from her.

Meet me downtown?

I had thought we wouldn't be able to meet up until after Christmas. My flight left on Friday night—the red-eye to JFK. Just the thought of seeing her gave me a little pick-me-up.

Sure. When and where?

Starbucks. Half an hour.

My heart did a little skip.

I've got class.

Yeah, so?

I'd never skipped school in my life. Even talking about it made my palms sweaty.

I've got a math quiz.

There was a long pause, and I thought I'd lost her. Then she messaged back.

If you don't want to meet up, just say so.

I really do have a quiz. How about after school?

I'm busy.

This time it was my turn to pause. What could I say without sounding like a nerd? And without pissing her off? I couldn't think of anything that didn't sound totally lame.

I can't just leave.

Say you're sick.

But I'm not sick.

Fake it!

I looked up and saw Sam and Riley watching me.

"What's up?" said Sam.

I think the blood must have rushed to my face, because suddenly I felt really hot.

"I'm not feeling so good," I said.

"Really? You were fine a minute ago," said Riley.

"It must have been that burger," I said, rubbing my stomach.

"Uh-huh," he said, nodding. "Funny, there wasn't anything wrong with mine."

I faked a grimace. "Lucky you."

"Who were you talking to?" said Sam.

"No one," I said quickly, then as an

afterthought added, "My mom. Flight details."

They nodded, clearly skeptical. As I said, I'm a crappy liar.

So are you coming or not?

I looked down at the phone and then up at Sam and Riley. They were still watching me.

"Seriously. I think I'm gonna puke," I said, holding my stomach and trying to sound sick. I probably just sounded pathetic. I stood up quickly, like I was going to run to the bathroom. "I'll see you guys later."

"Better brush up on your acting before you hit the office," Sam called after me.

I didn't bother responding, just rushed out of the cafeteria. Once out of sight, I slowed down and messaged Casey.

See you in half an hour.

Chapter Ten

Casey wasn't at Starbucks when I arrived. I knew I was late, but I couldn't believe she'd ditch me for a lousy five minutes. She'd waited longer than that for me before. I nabbed a seat by the window.

Five minutes turned into ten and then fifteen. I messaged her. No response. I waited a few more minutes, considering every scenario I could think of that might make her late. Finally I made myself face the truth. She'd stood me up. She wasn't coming.

Maybe she'd never planned on coming and it was all a big joke.

I left without buying anything and ambled down toward the water. If they'd been able to see me now, Sam and Riley would have no trouble believing I was sick. I felt like crap. I didn't want to believe Casey would play a prank like that on me. I thought we had more respect for each other. I knew I did for her. But did it go both ways? Again, it came down to the fact that I knew next to nothing about her.

The square in front of the Conference Center was almost deserted. I'd started to walk past when I heard voices. Voices raised in anger. I looked up and saw a couple of teenagers standing near the fountain, shouting at each other like a married couple on the verge of divorce. In each other's faces, arms waving. Even from this distance I could see that the girl was Casey.

I couldn't make out what they were saying, so I moved closer, staying in the shadows out of sight. Casey's voice was shrill, her cheeks flushed. She was giving as good as she was getting, but somehow I had the feeling she was on the defensive. The guy was aggressive, in her face. I watched for a couple of minutes, catching a word or a phrase now and then.

"...talk to the cops..." That was Casey, her voice shaky. With anger or fear, I wasn't sure.

"...know it was you...no one else..."

"...any one of them..." Casey again. "You know me..."

"...you're lying." The guy moved closer and stabbed Casey in the chest with his finger. She stumbled on the steps of the fountain, lost her balance and dropped down onto the concrete edge. The guy stood over her, fists clenched.

That was enough for me. I ran toward them.

"Hey, Casey!"

They both looked in my direction, and in a horrible, sinking moment of recognition I saw that the guy was Zane Bailey. Suddenly I found it difficult to breathe.

"There you are. Sorry I'm late," I said, stopping in front of them. The tightness in my chest made it easy to pretend I was out of breath from running.

"What the—?"

I tried to ignore Zane glowering down at me. He's easily over six feet tall and built like a quarterback. I felt like I had a pit bull breathing down my neck.

"I missed my bus, as usual," I said, focusing on Casey and edging closer to her so Zane had to back away a step. "Goddamn leg." I laughed, then looked up at Zane and did a double take.

"Zane Bailey?" Even to my ears it sounded fake, but there was no backing down now. "Hey, where've you been hanging? I haven't seen you in ages."

Zane glared at me, then at Casey. "Do you know this loser?"

It was the moment of truth. She would either go along with me or deny my very existence. I still didn't know which it would be. Then she slipped her arm through mine. I could feel the tension in her body as she leaned into me.

"Of course I do. Leon, Zane. Zane, Leon," she said in a parody of introduction.

"I know who he is," said Zane. "I just didn't think he'd be your type."

"We're not—I mean, we run together, that's all," I said. But Casey clutched my arm even harder.

"I told you I was on my way to meet someone," said Casey, her voice flat now, defiant. "You never believe me, do you, Zane?" I didn't think she was talking about me anymore.

"I'll start believing you when you start telling the truth," Zane said. "Don't forget, I've seen you in action."

"You've seen what you've wanted to see," Casey replied, anger creeping into her voice again.

"Don't tell me what—"

"You know," I said, "we should go. We're gonna be late for our—thing."

Zane turned his gaze to me, and I caught

a glimpse of raw emotion there that made me fear for Casey. And for myself. I backed away, trying to pull Casey with me. She stood her ground for a moment before yielding to my hand on her arm.

"You're right," she said. "We're late already. We wouldn't want to miss it." She glared at Zane for a moment longer, then turned and hurried away, dragging me along with her. We didn't look back.

Chapter Eleven

We walked in silence for a couple of blocks. I hadn't realized we were heading back to the Starbucks until Casey turned in the entrance. She ordered a double-shot caramelized-honey latte and then moved aside so I could order.

"Hot chocolate," I said

We waited for our drinks, then found a table. She still hadn't said anything to me. After I'd scooped the marshmallows out of my drink, I put my spoon down and took a deep breath.

"So, are you going to tell me what all that was about?" I said.

"All what?"

"That business with Zane Bailey."

She shrugged. "He's just a guy I know."

I raised my eyebrows. "I figured that much out for myself," I said.

"What do you want me to say? I ran into him on the way down here. He wanted to talk." She picked up her latte and cradled it in both hands. She wouldn't meet my gaze.

"Talk? That was an out-and-out shouting match."

"You're exaggerating," she said.

"Casey, he looked ready to belt you. What's going on?"

She put the drink down and sat back in her chair. "Okay. We used to go out, all right? It didn't end well."

"You went out with Zane Bailey?"

"Yeah, so?"

"So he's a low-life scumbag. What are you doing going out with a guy like that?"

"What kind of a guy do you want me to go out with? A guy like you?"

I shook my head, frustrated. "That's not what I meant. I just think you can do way better than Zane Bailey. He's trouble, Casey. Stay away from him."

"You're the dating police now?"

"No, but seriously, he's a dropkick. Stay away from him. I mean it."

She leaned toward me, her voice intense. "Don't tell me what to do, Leon. You don't own me. You don't even know me."

"I didn't mean it like that—"

"Well, what did you mean? Because it sounded pretty clear to me."

I sighed. "I just meant he's bad news. He's into all sorts of things—alcohol, drugs. He's been to juvie at least once that I know of."

She folded her arms across her chest. "Oh, so now you're an expert on Zane Bailey, are you?"

"No, but—"

"I think I'm in a better position to know what kind of a person he is, don't you?"

I couldn't answer that. I picked up my hot chocolate and gulped some down, trying to think of what to say. Casey stared out the window, fists clenched, silent.

"Look, it's none of my business, really—"

"No, it's not."

"But I saw you guys arguing and I was scared for you. He's a loose cannon."

"I can take care of myself."

"I'm sure you can," I said.

She turned to look at me, her eyes narrowed. "Believe me, Leon Kline, I've faced tougher situations than a fight with my ex-boyfriend. I don't need you or anyone else trying to swoop in and rescue me." She grabbed her coffee and stood to go.

A paper dropped out of her pocket and onto the floor. I bent down and picked it up, went to hand it to her, then saw the heading. It was a flyer for the half marathon at Santa Cruz, held every April.

"What's this?"

She glanced at it. "The reason I asked you to meet up in the first place. Thought you might be into training for it. I'm sure you're too busy rescuing damsels in distress though."

She slung her bag over her shoulder and left.

Chapter Twelve

Two days later I left for New York.

Seeing Grandma in a wheelchair hit me harder than I'd expected. She looked so old. Old and frail, like if I hugged her too hard she might break. I stood in the tiny living room, where the furniture had been shoved together to make room for the Christmas tree, and shuffled from one foot to the other, not knowing where to look or what to do.

"Don't just stand there, Leon," said Grandma. "Come and sit down. Talk to me." She patted the seat next to her wheelchair, the wingback chair by the window that had always been hers. No one ever sat in that chair but Grandma.

I chucked my bag in a corner and went and sat on the other side of her, on the couch next to Grandpa. He turned and looked at me with a kind of vacant stare.

"It's Leon, Dad," said Mom, taking off her coat and hanging it on the coatrack. "Your grandson."

"I know who he is," said Grandpa irritably. "What's he doing here?"

"He's here for the Christmas holidays, remember?" said Mom.

"No one told me he was coming," said Grandpa. "Why didn't you tell me he was coming? I would have met him at the airport." He looked accusingly at Mom and Grandma.

"Of course we told you, you goose," said Grandma. "You just forgot."

"I did not," said Grandpa. "I would have remembered that my grandson was coming to visit. Why doesn't anyone tell me what's going on anymore?"

Mom patted him on the shoulder. "It's okay, Dad. It must have slipped your mind, that's all."

"How was your flight, Leon?" said Grandma.

I shrugged, stifling a yawn. "It was all right."

"Are you tired? Do you want to lie down? Do you want some breakfast?" she said. "Mira, make the boy some eggs. He must be starving."

"No, I'm all right," I said. "They gave us breakfast on the plane."

She made a rude noise. "Airplane food. It's like eating cardboard. They should be ashamed to serve such garbage. Some toast, at least, and a hot chocolate. You can't say no to a hot chocolate, I'm sure."

Mom was already in the kitchen, and I heard eggs being cracked. "Mom, I'm not hungry, really," I called out. The apartment was so small you didn't need to yell.

"Not hungry," said Grandma. "You look like you haven't eaten in a week. He's so skinny."

"I know," said Mom, peering out from the kitchen. "That's what I said to him at the airport. And he's shot up another couple of inches, I'm sure. Have you been eating, Leon? Is your father feeding you?"

"Yes, Mom. Of course Dad's feeding me." Which wasn't exactly true. But I wasn't going to tell Mom that.

"How is your leg?" asked Grandma. "I couldn't believe it when I heard about your accident. In a running race? Who would have thought running was a dangerous sport?"

"It's fine," I said.

"Do you have much pain? The pain when I broke my hip was excruciating. And so slow to heal. I have some painkillers if you need them."

"No thanks, Grandma," I said. "It doesn't hurt anymore. I'm fine."

Mom came out of the kitchen with a steaming plate and set it on the dining table behind me. The smell of ham-and-cheese omelet hit my nostrils, and I was instantly starving.

"Come and eat something, Leon," she said. "I'm sure you're hungry. You're always hungry."

"Get him some toast, Mira," said Grandma. "He can't eat eggs without toast. And some strawberry jam. There's some in the cupboard."

I clambered out of the sofa cushions while Grandpa stared at me with suspicion.

"I would have met him at the airport," he grumbled.

My mom's a good cook, and the omelet was delicious. More important, it gave me something to do and an excuse not to join in the conversation, if you could call it that. I shoveled the chow into my mouth and listened to Grandma's inane chatter and wondered how I would get through the next two and a half weeks.

And I thought about Casey. I really wanted to send her a message right then, something witty about being trapped in an insane asylum or something. She'd get it. She'd send back an LOL or an emoticon or something, and I'd imagine her laughing, her head thrown back, exposing the burn on her neck that I hardly noticed anymore. But we hadn't spoken since that afternoon at Starbucks. I'd gone over our conversation hundreds of times, replayed it in my mind over and over, and I still didn't get it. She'd been so mad. What had I said that was so awful? That would make her not want to talk to me, not even to say goodbye?

I nodded and smiled when Grandma looked my way, and I thought about how to apologize to Casey when I didn't know what I'd done wrong in the first place. In the end, I sent her nothing. Because sending nothing and getting nothing was better than the alternative, sending something and getting nothing back. If I was never going to hear from her again, I didn't want to know about it.

Chapter Thirteen

The days dragged on, and I took to running. I had to do something, get out of the apartment or go crazy. Running in Brooklyn was totally different from running in Monterey. There were lots of people around, but no one knew me and no one wanted to know me. They minded their own business and were totally oblivious to a seventeen-year-old kid out for a run, limp or no limp.

The air was fresh and cold on my face, the pavement solid and comforting underfoot. Bon Jovi blasted through my earphones. I'd never liked Bon Jovi much, but Cascy had changed my mind. She never ran to anything else, and she was right. The music energized me. The rhythms pounded through my skull, keeping my feet in time. Even my limp seemed less pronounced when I ran to Bon Jovi. Okay, maybe I was just imagining it, but with Bon Jovi running through my head, I felt like Rocky Balboa.

I started out going a few blocks, twenty minutes max, and then I'd duck into a café or a 7-Eleven and hang out for a while to get out of the cold. Before long the run stretched out to thirty minutes, then forty-five. It felt good, and I could feel myself getting fitter, faster. Okay, not fast like I used to be, but faster than I'd been. I'd never be a sprinter again. That was obvious. But now I could go out on the street and pound the pavement without feeling like a total failure.

New Year's Eve was unusually warm. The temperature rose a good fifteen degrees, so it felt more like a cold day in California than New York at Christmastime. I pulled on a pair of track pants and a T-shirt and headed out.

The streets were crowded. Everyone was out doing last-minute shopping, having lunch, drinks, preparing for the night's festivities. I dodged through the foot traffic for a while, weaving from side to side, and stopping and starting until I came across a subway entrance. Mom was out with Grandma and Grandpa and not likely to be home anytime soon. There were better places to run. I headed down the stairs.

I hopped off at Brooklyn Bridge Park. The warm weather had brought out all the walkers and joggers and cyclists, and the people who just wanted to sit on the waterfront and enjoy the view. But despite the crowd, it was easy to slot through them and keep up a steady pace. I plugged in my headphones, cranked up the volume and drank in the views and the sea air while I chugged along with the other joggers.

For the first time since my accident, I felt like I belonged. I let the music lead my feet wherever they wanted to go. I didn't think about living in that tiny apartment with Grandma in her wheelchair and Grandpa slowly losing his mind. I didn't think about Sam and Riley and track, or Dad and his moody silence, or what I was going to do next year, or my stumpy leg, or even about Casey. I just ran. My arms and legs pumped away, and my lungs drew in the fresh, salty air. I was breathing hard but not too hard. Once I got into the rhythm, I could have gone on forever.

Of course, eventually I did get tired. I flopped down under a big tree at the north end of the park, near Pier 1. I could see Brooklyn Bridge stretching across the harbor, and I had a panoramic view of the skyscrapers of Lower Manhattan. It was spectacular. I sat and admired the view for a bit, until my stomach told me I hadn't eaten any lunch. I smelled hot dogs, the kind you only get in New York, and followed my nose until I found the place that was selling them.

It wasn't until lights started twinkling on in apartments and office buildings across the harbor that I realized how late it was. I glanced at the time on my phone, then swore under my breath. I made a beeline for the subway.

Half walking, half jogging, I dialed Mom's number. Busy. I hung up and dialed Grandma and Grandpa's. It rang for a long time. I was almost at the station when Grandpa answered.

"Grandpa, it's me, Leon," I said.

"Who?"

"Leon—you know, your grandson."

"I know who Leon is," said Grandpa. "He's my grandson. He lives in California. Who's this?"

"It's Leon," I said, my gut clenching. "Can I talk to Mom?"

"Leon? What are you doing calling long distance, boy?" said Grandpa. "Do you know how expensive that is? Money doesn't grow on trees, you know."

I groaned. This wasn't going well. "It's all right. The call isn't costing me anything. I'm here in New York, remember? Visiting for the Christmas holidays."

"I think I would know if my grandson was visiting," Grandpa said. He sounded irate, and I tried to stay calm. If I made him angry, I wouldn't get anywhere.

"Yeah, of course you would," I said. "I just need to talk to Mom."

"Your mother's not here," he said. "You're making no sense, boy. Are you feeling all right?"

"I'm fine, Grandpa," I said, heading down the steps into the subway. I'd lose the signal in a minute. "Look, if you talk to Mom, can you tell her I called and I'm on my way home?"

"Why would I be talking to your mother? What's going on?" He sounded anxious now.

I paused on the stairs, weighing the likelihood of getting my message through, then sighed. "Nothing's going on, Grandpa. Everything's fine. Don't worry. I'll talk to Mom myself."

"Yes, you do that. Thank you for calling," he said and hung up.

I stuffed the phone in my pocket and ran down the stairs. There'd be hell to pay when I got back.

Chapter Fourteen

It was full dark by the time I pushed open the door to Grandma and Grandpa's apartment. I'd tried to call once I got off the train, but by then my phone was dead. So I'd hurried home as fast as I could. I eased the door open and tried to sneak in quietly, but of course, in a place that small, a mouse would have a hard time getting in unnoticed.

Grandma spotted me first. "Mira, Leon's back, safe and sound. I told you not to worry."

Mom turned, said something quietly to whoever she'd been talking to on the phone and put it down before glaring at me.

"What did I tell you?" she said, hands on her hips. "Let me know where you're going and when to expect you back. Is that too much to ask?"

I scowled. "Sorry."

"Is it?"

"No, but I tried to call, Mom—"

"Well, you didn't try hard enough. I get home and you're gone? No note, no message. You don't answer your phone. What are we supposed to think?"

"I just went for a run."

"For four hours? What did you do, run to Manhattan and back?"

I smirked. I couldn't help it—she was that close to the truth.

"This is not funny, Leon. Anything could have happened." Her voice cracked. I was afraid she might cry.

"Mom, I'm seventeen, for God's sake. Stop treating me like a baby. What's gonna happen?"

"What's going to happen? How about getting mugged, for starters? Beaten up, murdered? This isn't Monterey, you know. It's New York. You can't just wander around anywhere you like at any time of the day or night. It's not safe, do you hear me?"

"Okay, enough, Mira," said Grandma. "It's not as bad as you're making out. You should know. You were a teenager here once yourself, remember?"

Mom ran a hand through her hair. "Yeah, that's the problem. I remember what it was like, and that was twenty-five years ago."

"I'm sorry I worried you, Mom," I said, feeling her backing down. "I lost track of the time. But I did call and tell Grandpa I was on my way back."

Mom turned to look at Grandpa, who so far had been sitting on the couch and watching what was going on without much interest.

"I called, didn't I, Grandpa?" I said. "Remember, I wanted to talk to Mom, but she wasn't here?"

"You didn't call. I would have remembered if you'd called," said Grandpa. He looked back and forth from me to Mom, then turned to Grandma. "You don't believe me, do you? You think I'm keeping secrets from you, but I tell you, no one called."

"It's all right, Dad," said Mom. "We believe you." She sounded tired now, defeated. I felt a bit guilty for worrying her. It couldn't be easy here, caring for Grandma and Grandpa. I'd only been here for a couple of weeks, and I felt like I was suffocating.

"I'm beat," I said. "I'm gonna hit the shower."

"I'll make you some supper," said Mom.

I stood in the shower and let the hot water run down my face. I had felt so good out there at the park, like a normal person again, and now I was back to feeling like crap. Guilty for worrying Mom, angry that I had to feel guilty, frustrated that she still treated me like a ten-year-old. I hadn't realized how much I'd got used to doing my own thing until I came here and she reined me in again. Surely she didn't think Dad was driving me around everywhere at home, keeping track of my movements, cooking and cleaning and doing the laundry. How could he? He was never home. And when he was, he didn't care what I did. Stay home, go out—it made no difference to him. He'd give me a grunt, or a "Yeah, have fun," if I was lucky. I could be out doing drugs or splashing graffiti around, and he would never know.

I heard the door handle rattle and a thud on the door.

"Almost done!" I said.

"Who's in there?" said Grandpa. Then, to someone on the other side, "The door is locked. I think someone is in there."

A knock on the door and Mom's voice. "Leon? Grandpa needs to use the bathroom."

"Just a minute!" I sighed and shut the water off, then grabbed a towel and wrapped it around my waist. "It's all yours,"

I said as I stomped past them, not caring that I was leaving wet footprints on the carpet. The sooner I got home, the better. Dad might not give a damn, but at least I had room to move.

I sat on Mom's bed, plugged my phone in and scrolled through my news feed. There were the usual updates from friends at school. Riley and Sam chilling out at the beach, Tyler West snowboarding at Whistler, Jo Perez and her sister at a family barbecue. Connor McDonald was visiting family in Scotland and had already posted pictures of the New Year's Eve fireworks.

Then a message came in from Pop. He's not the most tech-savvy person in the world and almost never texts me, so I was a little nervous as I opened it.

Leon. Pop here. Your dad won't be able to talk to you tonight like you planned. He was called in to work.

I wasn't sure if I was relieved or sorry. The Skype call with Dad at Christmas had been awkward to say the least. I didn't even know what to say to him anymore.

That's cool. Nothing too bad, I hope.
An abandoned warehouse near the recycle depot. It's been empty for years. Looks like there was some accelerant used. It went up like a torch.

I saw the words *recycle depot* and just about dropped the phone. There couldn't be two empty warehouses near there.

Was anyone hurt?
No. There were a bunch of beer bottles out the back but no one was there at the time.

I let out my breath.

Thanks for letting me know, I typed before he could get going on a rant. **Mom's got dinner ready. I'll see you soon.**

I stared at the phone, my fingers itching to message Casey. It had to be the same warehouse. There just weren't that many empty warehouses in that area. What if she'd been in there when it went up? What if she'd fallen asleep or something, or had even had a few too many beers and passed out? Would they find her body?

Don't be an idiot, I told myself. No one was there when the fire started. No one was hurt. Pop would know. He always knows. But I kept seeing Casey slipping through the sliding doors into the warehouse and couldn't get rid of the niggling doubt that maybe he was wrong.

I stewed on it for hours, through Mom's chicken stir-fry, through Grandpa forgetting he'd already eaten and asking when dinner would be ready, through the whole of *New Year's Rockin' Eve* that Grandma insisted on watching right through to the ball drop. When the fireworks went off, I took a Snapchat photo, typed **Happy New Year** and sent it to Casey. She didn't open it, and she didn't message back.

Chapter Fifteen

I didn't hear from her until I got home. I was in English, and Mr. Pearce was going on about *Romeo and Juliet*. Something about loyalty and feuding. I was almost asleep. My phone vibrated in my pocket. I snuck it out to have a look.

> **Welcome home, stranger. Hope you had a good trip.**

That was it. No mention of the argument we'd had, no apology for the long silence. *Welcome home, stranger*. Like it was my fault we hadn't been talking.

Like I hadn't been worrying about her for the last five days, imagining her burned to a crisp in that building. Well, two could play that game. If she wanted to pretend like nothing had happened, then that's how we'd play it.

The best trip ever. Nothing beats New York at Christmas.

She didn't need to know I'd spent every minute wishing I was in Monterey.

Saw your photos on Facebook. The fireworks looked amazing.

I stared at the message. She hadn't needed to go to Facebook to see those fireworks. Why hadn't she opened the Snapchat?

They were. Better than any I've ever seen.

How cool was Times Square? I would give anything to actually be there and see the ball drop live.

I paused again. If she'd seen the photos on Facebook, she would know I hadn't been to Times Square at all. I'd watched it on TV like everyone else. The fireworks I'd posted had been the ones at Prospect Park, which wasn't that far away from Grandma and Grandpa's apartment building and could be seen from their window.

Sam kicked me under the desk, and I looked up to see Mr. Pearce watching me. I turned the page in my book and hunched over it, like I was really concentrating. He turned to the whiteboard and got back to *Romeo and Juliet*. I waited about a minute and texted Casey.

It was awesome. Can't talk. Are we on for a run Saturday morning?

A pause, then:

Gotta work off these holiday pounds somehow. The usual time and place. See you there.

See you—

A hand reached over my shoulder and took the phone out of my grasp.

"You can retrieve this at the end of the day, Leon," said Mr. Pearce. "After you write me a five-hundred-word essay on the class discussion today."

A snigger rippled through the class, and I sank down into my seat.

"I tried to warn you," said Sam later as we stood in line at the cafeteria.

I shrugged. "Who cares? Everyone gets detention."

"Yeah? Not me," said Sam. "I get detention and I'm off the track team."

"Well, I don't have to worry about that anymore, do I," I said, scooping up a plate of fries.

Sam slammed a sandwich onto his tray. "You know, you really need to get rid of that chip on your shoulder."

I turned and looked at him. "What are you talking about?"

He paused, then shook his head. "Nothing."

I followed him over to a table.

"No, not nothing," I said. "You can't say something like that and then just expect me to drop it."

"You want the truth?"

"Yeah."

"Really? You're sure?"

"Give it to me, Sam. You've obviously been stewing on this for a while."

He took a bite of his sandwich and stared at me, chewing a long time before swallowing.

"Okay, look. I know you've had a hard time with your leg and everything, but the truth is, you're no fun anymore. You mope around here, dragging your feet, sulking every time we even mention track, on your phone twenty-four/seven. You're ditching school and getting detention. What's happened to you?"

"Nothing," I said, looking down at my fries. I picked one up and ate it without tasting it. "What are you, my mother?"

"You see? That's exactly what I'm talking about," said Sam.

"What do you want me to say? You want me to be all cheery, like oh, sorry, Sam, for not being the life of the party, for putting a damper on your perfect life, it's just that my own life is going down the toilet and there's not one damn thing I can do about it."

I was panting like I'd run a 100-meter sprint. I pushed the plate of fries away and glared at Sam.

"Your life isn't going down the toilet," he said.

I threw my hands up. "What would you call it then? I can't run, I can't do track, my chance of going to college is next to zero. Even my parents have given up on me."

"They haven't."

"They have. At least my dad has."

A pause while he digested this.

"You should come back to track, Leon," he said.

I rolled my eyes. "That's not the answer. Honestly? I don't even care that much about track anymore."

"It's not about track," said Sam. "It's about hanging out with your friends, having something to do, a purpose. It doesn't matter if you're crap. The whole team is crap this year. It won't matter if you don't win."

I snorted. "Thanks. I think I'll pass." I shoved my chair back and left.

Chapter Sixteen

Saturday morning I got the early bus to the park. I'd been mulling over what Sam had said, and he was right. Not about track. I would never go back to that. But about having a purpose. Before the accident I'd had goals—making the first-string team, finishing school, getting an athletics scholarship and going to college. Since I'd broken my leg, I'd been drifting. I needed a focus. And Casey might just give me one.

She hadn't put on any holiday pounds. If anything, she looked thinner, stressed out.

There were hollows in her cheeks I hadn't noticed before and dark circles under her eyes. Her hair was blue.

"Hey, Gilburn!" she said, sauntering up. "Long time no see."

I wanted to hug her. She seemed fragile somehow. Insubstantial. I held back the urge and gave a stupid half salute instead.

"Yeah, it's been a while," I said, then dug my hands in my pockets as I searched for something else to say. "How was your Christmas?"

Her face closed over. Wrong thing to ask.

"It was fine," she said. "Are we gonna run or not?"

"Ready when you are," I said, grinning like a demonic clown.

She did a couple of stretches, then turned and headed out of the park. I followed her, wishing I could swallow my tongue and start fresh. It was like I'd forgotten how to talk over the holidays. Too much time spent with Grandpa. Just chill out, I told myself. Stop trying so hard.

We ran two or three blocks then turned toward the beach. It was at least five miles to the ocean, and I waited for her to turn down another side street and circle around back to the park. She just kept running, though, checking back over her shoulder now and then. It was almost like she was pushing me to see if I would quit, waiting for me to call out, tell her I needed to stop. I didn't do it. She kept going, and I kept plodding along after her like a faithful puppy. At last I got a whiff of salt air, and then we were there, near the beach at Fisherman's Wharf. She slowed to a walk, then stopped, hands on her knees, breathing hard.

"You've been running," she said.

I was puffing, walking circles around her, trying not to show how much I hurt.

"Yeah." *Pant, pant.* "Every day."

"Impressive," she said. Slowly she straightened, stretched her arms up.

"Oh God, I'm done," I said and dropped to the ground.

She laughed. That amazing fountain of sound that transformed her. I had to laugh with her, not an easy thing when I was gasping for air like an asthmatic goldfish.

She pulled me up, and we strolled down to the beach.

"So how was it really?" she said. "In New York. You didn't fool me with your *best holiday ever* routine."

I snorted noncommittally. "Should have known you wouldn't buy that."

"You're a lousy liar, Leon, even by text."

I shrugged. "You're right. It wasn't the best holiday ever. Grandma and Grandpa are...old. Like, really old. I didn't expect that."

"Why not? They're your grandparents. That makes them old by definition."

I sat on a log and stared out at the ocean. The tide was out, and waves lapped gently on the wet sand.

"They've always been old, obviously, but they used to be...I don't know...capable. Now they rely on Mom for everything. Grandma's in a wheelchair because of her broken hip, and Grandpa..."

"What?"

"He's just not himself anymore. He forgets things, like, all the time. You tell him something, and two minutes later he asks you the very same thing. Over and over again. He's cranky and irritable. Half the time he just seems confused."

"Maybe he has Alzheimer's."

I swiveled around to look at her. "What?"

"Alzheimer's disease. You know, dementia."

They were the words I hadn't been able to bring myself to say. Not to anyone, not even myself.

I thought back to the things Grandpa had done, the things he'd said or not said. The look of hurt and confusion that would cross his face when you expected him to remember something that had happened. The misplacing of items, the accusations that Grandma was making things up to make him look bad, the apartment door that was always locked.

But surely Mom would have told me if he had Alzheimer's. That was serious, right? People died from Alzheimer's.

Was Grandpa dying and no one had even bothered to tell me?

"I'm sure it's not," said Casey. "Forget I mentioned it. I haven't even met your grandfather. What would I know?"

"Yeah. I'm sure it's nothing," I said. "He's just forgetful. Everyone gets forgetful when they get old."

"Exactly," said Casey.

We fell silent. Seagulls squawked overhead. A little kid ran behind us with her dog, laughing as it dragged her along. Casey pulled her phone out and started playing with it. I couldn't get thoughts of Grandpa out of my mind.

"Okay, so do you want to hear about a funny thing that happened?" she said finally.

That got my interest.

"I was at this party on Christmas Eve. At Jake Bellamy's place. Do you know Jake?"

I shook my head.

"He's a senior at Newbury. Anyway, he's got this huge place, like fifteen bedrooms or something, a pool and a tennis court, stables, the whole bit. Everyone from school was there, except maybe Harvey Miller. He never goes anywhere."

I smiled.

"So we're out by the pool, me and Shania and Zane and Marty and a couple of others."

The mention of Zane's name made my insides churn, but I kept quiet.

"We've had a few drinks and the music's pretty good and we're kinda groovin' a bit— you know how it is."

I nodded, although I didn't know. I'd always been the Harvey Miller of Gilburn. Until this year anyway.

"So along comes Jake's little sister, Alice, and she is smashed. She's got a cup of punch in her hand, and she's slurping it down like it's Kool-Aid. Maybe she thought it was Kool-Aid, I don't know."

"How old is she?"

"I don't know—fourteen, fifteen, maybe. That's not the point." She frowned at me, and I nodded for her to go on. "So she comes staggering over, and I know something's up. She sidles right up to Zane, and she starts singing this sappy love song to him."

I shake my head in disbelief.

"Do you know 'You Light Up My Life'?"

"I've heard of it," I said. I wasn't going to admit it was my mom's favorite song.

"Sappiest song on the planet," she said. "I was so embarrassed for her. And for Zane. Oh my god, he looked like he wanted to crawl into a hole and disappear."

I laughed. I could totally picture Zane squirming.

"All of a sudden she stops singing and turns absolutely green. She drops her cup and runs. I think she meant to run into the bushes to upchuck, but she goes the wrong way and falls straight into the pool!"

Casey's laughing so hard she can barely get the story out. It's infectious, and I'm laughing too, even though it's not that funny.

"She's floundering around, and I'm scared she's gonna drown, so I jump in after her without even thinking, shoes, purse, drink and all." She shook her head. "What an idiot I am."

"Yeah, good one, Casey. Real smart." I wiped my eyes.

"At least I got her out."

"You're right. Absolutely." I chuckled again, and then, when the laughter had died down, gave her a sideways glance. "So is that when you lost your phone?"

She looked at me sharply, all trace of laughter erased. "How did you know I lost my phone?"

I shrugged. "It's not rocket science. I sent you a Snapchat on New Year's Eve that you never opened. Then, when I saw your phone..." I gestured toward the iPhone in her hand. "That's new, isn't it?"

She grinned, visibly relaxed. It made me wonder what she'd been afraid of.

"You're a regular detective, aren't you?"

"I do my best." I didn't push it. I was just glad we were talking again. "Hey," I said. "Do you still want to do the race at Santa Cruz?"

"The what?"

"The half marathon. Remember?" I pulled the brochure out of my pocket and unfolded it.

She took the paper from me and smoothed it out on her leg. "I'd totally forgotten about this," she said.

"We should do it."

She turned to look at me, all serious at first, and then her eyes crinkled at the corners. "You sure you're up for it?"

I laughed. "Maybe not the half marathon, but the 10K. Absolutely."

She paused a second longer, and then the smile flooded her face. "Okay, Gilburn. You're on."

Chapter Seventeen

The next few weeks went by slowly. The weather was cold and mostly clear, and the news was filled with stories about the lack of rain and talk of drought. Homework ramped up at school, and final exams loomed closer. Everyone was talking about graduation, but I couldn't get excited about it. Not when the future beyond June was so uncertain.

I ran every day before school, and Casey and I trained every weekend. I still couldn't keep up to her, but at least I wasn't a total wreck when we finished. I started putting on some muscle and I stopped eating junk food. That was a biggie. Even Dad noticed when he came home one day to find me making grilled chicken with salad instead of mac and cheese. Not that he said anything much. Just kinda looked and nodded and asked if there was enough for two. There wasn't, but I shared it anyway, and we both pretended we weren't still hungry.

Casey, on the other hand, was getting thinner and thinner. The running was taking off pounds she didn't have to lose, and it didn't look like she was eating. Not regularly anyway. It crossed my mind that maybe she was anorexic, but whenever I brought a snack to have after our run, she gobbled it down like she was starving. Maybe she was. I just had no idea why. And aside from opening up about that Christmas party, she was as tight-lipped as ever, and no amount of good-natured teasing could get her to spill any other secrets.

Just before spring break I was about to head out to meet her for our usual training session when Mom called.

"I've got some news," she said. "I'll be home at the end of the month."

"That's great," I said. "So Grandma's better? They don't need you to look after them anymore?"

There was a long pause. We were on Skype, and I could see Mom biting her lip, her eyes flicking over to something or someone outside of the screen. I heard Grandma's voice, quiet and serious.

"Just tell him, Mira. He's a grown boy. He deserves to know."

The words slipped through me, sharp and quick and deep.

"What's going on, Mom?" I said.

Mom took a deep breath. "Grandma and Grandpa are going to live in a nursing home," she said.

"What?" I paused for a second while the words registered in my brain. "Why? I thought Grandma was getting better.

You said she was walking now, on crutches." I sounded like a whiny ten-year-old, but I couldn't help it.

"She is," said Mom. "But she's not well enough to look after Grandpa on her own."

"Maybe not yet, but soon, right?" I don't know why it was so important to me. Lots of people lived in nursing homes. It's what you did when you were old.

"No, I'm afraid not, Leon," said Mom. "The truth is, Grandpa's memory loss is getting worse. He needs more help than we can provide at home. Professional help."

I stared at her through the screen, a massive weight filling my stomach. "It's Alzheimer's, isn't it?"

Her shoulders relaxed, like a load had been taken off. "Yes, it is."

"How long have you known?"

"I've suspected for a long time," said Mom. There was resignation in her voice, sorrow. It suddenly hit me that we weren't just talking about my grandpa. We were talking about her dad. "But Grandpa refused to go to the doctor, and Grandma didn't push him. We only got confirmation last month."

"Why didn't you tell me? At Christmas when I was there?"

Mom shook her head sadly. "We didn't know for sure then, and besides, there was nothing you could have done."

Except maybe I would have been nicer to him. Maybe I wouldn't have grumbled under my breath every time he forgot something or asked the same question twice or switched the TV channel looking for the show that had just ended. Maybe I wouldn't have blamed him for not passing on messages to Mom or for moving my phone and forgetting where he'd put it. Maybe I would have been a little more patient.

"I'm sorry, Mom," I said.

"Oh, Leon," she said and burst into tears.

Grandma came onto the screen, crutches tucked under her armpits. She put her arms around Mom.

"Don't you worry about us," she said. "We'll be fine. Your mom's found us a nice place not far from here. We'll have a little apartment and people to help us. There's a games room and a coffee shop, and it's a secure building, so we don't have to worry about Grandpa wandering off like he did last week."

"Grandpa wandered off? Where did he go?"

Grandma gave Mom's arm a squeeze. "He just went to get some milk, but once he was out, he got a bit confused about where he was."

Grandpa had lived in that neighborhood all his life. This was serious.

"Okay, I get it. Grandpa needs help, but why do you have to go too?"

Grandma's face took on a cloak of sadness and exhaustion. "Leon, I'm getting back on my feet, but I can't manage on my own. Quite frankly, I don't want to manage on my own. Grandpa and I have been together for more than fifty years. Besides, we could never afford both places."

Mom took a shaky breath and straightened her shoulders. "We've thought it all through, Leon. Really. This is the best solution. Everyone thinks so—Grandma, me, your father."

"Dad knows?"

"Of course he does. Look, we'll talk more when I get back. I'll stay until they're settled in at the end of the month. It won't be long."

She said goodbye, and I closed the laptop. I wasn't sure what to think about the news. I knew it made sense. But somehow my heart was rebelling. Grandma and Grandpa were moving out of the home they'd lived in all their lives. Where I'd visited them year after year. Thanksgiving dinners crowded around the tiny dining table, watching television squashed between them on the couch, walking with them in Central Park. None of that would happen anymore.

And Grandpa had Alzheimer's. I didn't know much about it, but I knew he'd never be the same again. Would we ever have another game of chess? Or watch the latest

Bourne movie together? Or go to a game at Yankee Stadium? Would he even recognize me next time I visited?

I got up from the desk and turned around. Dad was standing in the doorway.

"Leon—"

"You could have told me," I said and pushed past him.

"Why? What good would that do?" he said, following me into the living room.

I grabbed my stuff off the couch. "Because he's my grandfather. I should know. I'm part of this family. Or have you forgotten?"

"Don't be ridiculous. Of course you're part of this family," he said.

"Really? You could have fooled me."

He threw his hands up. "This is exactly why I didn't tell you, Leon. Because I knew you'd react like this. What do you want? Someone to pat you on the back and tell you everything will be okay?"

I headed for the door.

"That's not the real world, Leon. It's time you grew up and stopped hiding behind your mother's skirts. The real world is a lion's den. You need to be a survivor. No one's going to sugarcoat things for you. The world will hit you over the head, and you need to just get back up again and keep going."

I spun around, hand on the door handle. "Great advice, Dad. Thanks. Are you speaking from personal experience or just making it up as you go along?" I was panting like I'd already done 10K on the track. "Because right now you're the last person I'm going to take advice from."

The door slammed behind me.

Chapter Eighteen

I was still fuming when I walked into the park to meet Casey. I'd considered not going at all, but I wouldn't give Dad the satisfaction of ruining my day. As it was, I was half an hour late, and I wouldn't have blamed Casey if she'd left without me. There she was, though, sitting on a picnic table in shorts and a T-shirt despite the cool breeze.

"I was beginning to think you wouldn't show," she said, looking up from her phone.

"Don't ask."

She grinned. "Trouble in paradise?"

I just shook my head and started stretching.

"If you don't want to talk about it, just say so," she said.

"I don't." I grabbed my foot and stretched my quad.

She shrugged and climbed off the table. "Let's go then," she said, setting off north.

I pounded after her, stump-step-stump-step-stump-step. I'd run like that for so long now, I usually didn't even notice it anymore. Today it rang in my ears, the off-beat rhythm drumming Dad's words into my head. Where did he get off telling me what to do? Giving me advice after all this time? After months and months of silence and indifference, now he decided he knew what was best for me? Who did he think he was? Dad of the Year? It was too late for that. Way too late.

I let my anger drive my feet and flew after Casey like we were running a marathon, like it was the final push to the finish line and winner take all. We passed a school and a corner shop and a gas station, then stopped at a crosswalk.

Casey glanced over at me as we jogged on the spot. Sweat glistened on her forehead, and she rubbed it away with the pressure sleeve on her arm.

"You're fast today, Gilburn."

I shrugged and turned to watch the light. As soon as it went green, I took off in the lead.

The thing was, my dad might be right. I didn't want to admit it, but once the idea popped into my head, I couldn't get rid of it. Was I looking for the easy way out? Looking for someone to tell me what to do, to take over the decision making? Avoiding thinking about graduation and hoping it would all work out okay? And if I was, so what? Who said I had to make a decision right now anyway? I was only seventeen. What was the big deal? It wasn't like you magically morphed into an adult on the day of graduation. Mom and Dad wouldn't kick me out the moment I finished school.

Or would they? Would Dad? Would his tough love extend that far?

It wasn't something I'd contemplated before. Not until this morning. Now it seemed like anything could happen. Come summer, I could be on the streets.

I saw the 7-Eleven up ahead where we'd said we'd finish the run. It was still a few hundred meters away, but I started sprinting. Casey was right behind me. I could hear her breathing, her feet hitting the pavement. I pumped my arms, pushed harder, felt my face screwing up into that weird look I used to have when I was running sprints. My lungs burned for oxygen, and my legs were screaming. I ignored them all and forced myself to keep going, not to give up. I wouldn't give up.

I reached the 7-Eleven and collapsed on the sidewalk in front of the glass doors. They slid open silently, then closed again. Casey jogged up, ten or twenty seconds behind me. Her face was red, the scars on her neck pale and silvery in comparison. She put her hands on her knees, panting, before looking up at me.

"You're nuts, do you know that?"

I climbed to my feet, my legs shaking. "I thought we were training. You can't just be fit, you know. You have to train for the finish."

"Right," she said, still panting.

I went in and bought two bottles of water, and we sat at a picnic table on a little patch of grass at the back of the parking lot. There was a tin ashtray full of butts on the table and an empty chocolate-milk carton underneath.

"So you were right," I said, without waiting for her to start the conversation. "My grandpa's got Alzheimer's."

She nodded, took a swig of her water. "That sucks."

"Yeah."

She waited a minute, then squinted at me in the sunlight. "So that's what's got you so bummed this morning?"

"Kinda."

"Kinda?"

I took a deep breath and blew it out. "I had a fight with my dad."

"Welcome to the club," she said. The bitterness in her voice surprised me, startled me out of my own mood. I wanted to ask her what she meant. What was going on in her life, why she was so thin, so hungry, and why she'd gone out without a hoodie and was now shivering in the breeze cutting across the parking lot. But her face was expressionless. Like a mask. One day it would crack, and I would have my opening. But not today.

"Do you think I'm a sissy?" I said instead.

She burst out laughing. "A sissy? Where did that word come from, 1960?"

"You know what I mean. Do you think I'm soft? Do I seem like the kind of person who gets handed everything?"

She tried to straighten her face, keep the laughter out of her voice.

"Soft? No, I wouldn't say soft exactly." Another giggle, quickly quashed. "I think maybe in the past you were babied a bit, but now?"

She turned and studied me seriously.

"You've changed a lot this year, Leon. You're not the kid I met in the waiting room at the physio. That kid would have seen the 7-Eleven and slowed down, walked the last few steps, said he was too tired to keep running, probably wouldn't have made it this far in the first place. But not now. You saw the finish line and you went for it, no matter how much it hurt. And believe me, I know you were hurting 'cause I was too. I'm still hurting."

She groaned and stretched one leg out, pointing and flexing her foot.

"I'm going to feel it tomorrow," she said. She put her arms up over her head, stretched up and then leaned forward over the table. It made her shirt ride up, exposing smooth white flesh and a large yellowing bruise on her lower back.

"What's that?" I said before I could stop myself.

She sat up quickly, pulling her shirt down. "What's what?"

"That bruise on your back. Who gave you that bruise?"

"No one *gave* me that bruise, Leon," she said, her eyes like ice picks. "I slipped and fell against a table, that's all."

I watched her face and she watched mine. I knew she was lying. And she knew I knew. But would I be foolish enough to call her out? To accuse Zane Bailey to her face? I'd seen him threaten her before. It had to be him. But the last time I'd said something against Zane, she hadn't spoken to me for a month.

"You should be careful," I said. "That looks like it hurt."

"It did." She looked away, and the tension left her body. "So, what do you think about Huckleberry Hill?"

"What do you mean?"

"As a training run," she said. "If you want to up the ante a bit, that'll definitely test your fitness."

I nodded. "That's a good idea. If we can do Huckleberry Hill, we'll be able to do

Santa Cruz easy. I saw the race route. There aren't many hills at all."

"All right. It's a plan." She pulled her phone out and looked at the time. "I gotta meet someone. I'll see you next week." She drained her water, hopped up and headed off.

I watched her go, her body appearing small and childlike as the distance increased. It was a long time before I thought about Grandpa's Alzheimer's and my fight with Dad again.

Chapter Nineteen

Huckleberry Hill Nature Preserve isn't far from the center of Monterey. I was surprised to find we had the place to ourselves, although it was early. Barely light. The trail to the top is only a couple of miles long, but steep, winding through the trees up the mountain.

We started at Quarry Park to make the run a little longer. Casey took the lead, like she usually did, but after a few minutes I sprinted to catch up and ran alongside her. She glanced over at me, didn't say anything, and we jogged along the dirt track, pacing ourselves, knowing what was ahead.

The trail took us through some deep woods, through a canyon and then past a bunch of houses near Veterans' Memorial Park. So far it was pretty easy. Although the footing wasn't as good as running on the pavement, the trail was quiet and peaceful, and I found myself relaxing into the rhythm of the run like I had at Brooklyn Bridge Park. Casey jogged along beside me, and it was as if we'd been running partners for years.

At Veterans' Park we headed into the nature preserve and started up Huckleberry Hill. That's where things got tough. I knew there was a brutal stair climb, but I hadn't realized just how long and steep it was. When she saw it, Casey turned and gave me this wicked grin, daring me to bail. I grinned back and started up the steps.

I lost count at 125. I was walking by then, dragging my bad leg. I still couldn't see the top, but there was no way I was going to quit. I kept my eyes down and just kept dogging it, one step at a time.

When I reached the top, Casey was waiting for me.

"Almost there," she said and headed off down the trail.

I wanted to collapse, to lie in the dirt and never get up again, or at least not for an hour or so. I took a couple of deep breaths, watching Casey moving steadily away from me, and then set off after her. She was right. It wasn't far. Only another half mile or so to the summit. And the hard slog was over.

I had trouble getting my legs going again. My rhythm was gone, and it took all my willpower to maintain some semblance of a jog. Casey moved farther and farther away until I could barely make her out in the trees. The thought of walking the rest of the way was tempting. I'd done the hard bit. Who would know if I walked or jogged the last half mile? Me for one. And Casey for two. We'd said we'd run the whole way if it killed us. Because when it came to Santa Cruz, we weren't giving up.

So I pushed myself through the pain, the burning in my thighs, the ache in my bad leg. I sucked air into my lungs and just thought about putting one foot in front of the other. When I looked up, I saw Casey sitting on a fence rail overlooking the city. It was like seeing the finish line in a 100-meter sprint. My heart lifted, and I felt a surge of energy. Where it came from I have no idea. I thought I'd used up all my reserves, but I was wrong. Before I knew it my arms were pumping and my head was back and I was going for the big finish.

When I reached the fence, I hung over the rail, blowing like a racehorse. That last adrenaline surge was still pumping through my veins, and I grinned and laughed through my gasping breaths.

"I can't believe we made it," I said.

"You can't believe *you* made it," said Casey. "I've been here for ages."

But I could see her chest was still heaving, sweat dripping off her brow. She was putting on a good show, but I wasn't fooled.

"All right then," I conceded. "I can't believe *I* made it."

We admired the view for a few minutes, catching our breath, then wandered off the path into the trees, sprawling on the ground in a small clearing. Casey picked at the dry grass. She seemed unusually quiet, nodding or smiling now and then while I complained about my dad and school and the guys. It was obvious she wasn't listening, so eventually I just shut up.

We sat in silence for a while. The woods were quiet, no voices, no footsteps, just a few birds twittering in the canopy above us. And then Casey spoke.

"Do you ever feel like giving up?" she said without looking at me. She said it casually, calmly, but something in her voice told me this wasn't a casual question.

"Of course," I said. "I sure felt like giving up halfway up those steps."

She pursed her lips. Didn't smile. Just shook her head slowly.

"I can't do it anymore, Leon," she said.

I sat up, on alert now. "Can't do what anymore?"

"I'm done dealing with everything. Dealing with *him*."

She still hadn't looked at me. My heart was thumping against my ribs. "Is Zane threatening you again? Did he hurt you?"

Her head came up, and she met my gaze. "Stop blaming everything on Zane, Leon. I'm not talking about him. He hasn't done anything. In fact, he's the only thing that's held me together these past couple of years. He gets me. He's the only one who gets me."

"Okay, okay," I said. "I'm sorry. I shouldn't have jumped to conclusions."

"No, you shouldn't have." She lapsed into silence again.

I sat back, cursing myself. Here she was, finally opening up, and I blew it. I knew I should just keep my trap shut, but I couldn't help myself.

"If not Zane, then who?" I asked.

She was quiet for so long I thought she was going to ignore the question. And it would serve me right for being an idiot. Eventually she took a deep breath and exhaled slowly.

"Robert," she said, and when I looked confused, "My stepfather."

I nodded. That I could relate to. "You don't get along?"

She laughed, a harsh barking sound, not her usual trill of delight. "He's a jerk. An absolute loser. I hate him." The venom in her voice was palpable.

"What happened?"

She raised her eyes and looked into the trees above us, shaking her head. "What hasn't happened? Everything. Nothing. At least nothing that hasn't been going on since my mom married him. I do something he doesn't like, we fight. I yell, he yells back. He is so controlling."

"Did he hit you?" I asked, almost afraid to hear the answer. "Is that where you got that bruise?"

She shrugged. "It wasn't anything much. He grabbed me. Tried to stop me from leaving, and I smashed into the door. But I'm not a puppet. I won't be his puppet. He can't tell me what to do and when to do it, who I can see or not see, what time I have to be home. It's my life, and he needs to get the hell out of it!"

She was shaking with anger, which scared me but was preferable to the quiet apathy she'd started out with.

"What are you going to do?" I asked.

"I don't know," she said, quieter now. "I can't stay there. Not with him."

"You could stay with me," I said, needing to do something, to help her in some way. "Just for a few days, until things settle down."

She smiled at me like I was a puppy begging for attention. "You're sweet, Leon. Thanks, but no."

She fell quiet and started picking at the grass again. I didn't know what to say. Or even if I should say anything. I felt useless when all I wanted to do was fix it for her.

"Do you know," she said, "power is a funny thing. Robert thinks he has all the power. That he can control everything in his life. He controls everything at his business, he controls my mom and Oscar, he controls all the money, the house. But power is an illusion. Power can shift, and he has no power over me. I won't let him have power over me."

"Good," I said. "He's a bully. Don't give in to him."

She glanced sideways at me and smiled. It wasn't a pleasant smile.

"Do you want to know how I take my power back?"

I was confused, but I nodded.

She studied my face for a moment and seemed satisfied with what she saw. "Let me show you."

There was a bunch of loose grass in front of her from her pulling at it, brown and dry and brittle. She gathered the bits of grass into a pile and then pulled a pack of matches out of her pocket.

"What are you doing?" I said.

"Just watch." She struck a match.

"Casey, no!"

Before I could grab her arm, she'd dropped the flaming match into the pile of dry grass. I reached for it, but she held me back. The grass caught.

"Just watch," she said, pushing me away, staring at the flame as it grew. "Watch it, Leon. It's power. Pure, raw power. Don't you see? He has no power over me. He can't control me."

I jumped up and stamped on the fire. Sparks flew up from under my foot. "You're nuts," I said. "The whole park will go up."

"Let it go, Leon," said Casey. "Can't you feel the power?"

I turned around. She'd struck another match and was carefully feeding another pile of grass.

"Stop! Casey!" I ran over and stomped on the new flame.

She darted away, struck a third match and dropped it in the grass. And a fourth.

I grabbed the matches from her.

The first fire hadn't completely gone out and was growing by the second, the third and fourth catching quickly. I had nothing to douse them with. Our water was gone. I put out the smallest of the fires and ran to the next, but already the heat coming off it was scorching, the flames spreading, fanned by the breeze. There was no way to get them all.

Casey stood nearby, quietly watching. Her face was calm, the fire reflected in her eyes. It was the calm that frightened me. That the fire could soothe her so.

I grabbed her hand and pulled her away. She resisted, backing up slowly, eyes locked on the fire. But I gave her arm a strong jerk, and she turned and looked at me.

"I'm sorry," she said. "I had to do it."

I didn't say anything, just dragged her behind me, racing for the steps. I was confused, angry, scared. And not just because of the fire rapidly growing behind us, but because of what I'd seen in Casey's face. Because somehow, at some level, it all made sense.

Chapter Twenty

We made it down the hill in record time. At the entrance to the park, a young family was starting up the trail, a mom and a dad and two young kids, one strapped in a pack on the dad's back.

"Fire!" I yelled. "There's a fire at the summit."

The mom snatched up the kid, and we ran the rest of the way down the trail together, the dad dialing 9-1-1 as we went. I don't know why I hadn't done that already. All I'd thought about was putting out the fires and then getting the hell out of there.

"They're on their way," he said when we reached the parking lot. "Get in—we'll give you a ride."

The mom already had one kid in the car and was dragging the other one out of the pack. I hesitated, turning to look for Casey.

"Get in," the dad repeated.

"But—" Casey was nowhere in sight. She'd vanished.

"I said, get in."

The man was tall, bulky and standing way too close to me. I backed away, and he grabbed my arm.

"You're not going anywhere, punk. I saw those matches in your hand. Now get in the car."

I looked down at the book of matches I'd taken off Casey. "It's not what you think," I said. "I didn't start that fire."

"Save it for the cops." He opened the passenger door and shoved me in, banging my head on the roof of the car in the process.

"Mark, get us out of here," said the mom from the backseat.

He didn't answer, just slammed the door and ran around to the driver's side. The car roared to life, tires squealing as we took off down the road. I squinted through the window as we drove, looking for Casey. There was no sign of her.

I gave my statement to the police, as did the dad and the mom, and that was the end of it. Until Pop came knocking on the door while we were eating dinner.

The kitchen seemed close and hot. I could feel Dad's eyes boring into me, along with Pop's and those of the sergeant he'd brought with him from the police station.

"I told you already. I didn't do it." I slouched farther into my chair, arms crossed over my chest as if to contain the thumping of my heart.

Dad leaned over the table, in my face. He smelled of smoke, like he always does when he's been out at a fire. "You were found with the bloody matches in your pocket.

You want us to believe they jumped out and lit the fire themselves?"

"David." Pop pulled Dad away from the table. "Let Sergeant Lewis handle it."

Dad shook off Pop's hand and went to stand in the doorway, glaring at me. The fire had been contained quickly. And no one had been hurt. I still felt guilty as hell, though, and Dad getting in my face wasn't making things any better.

"Tell me again why you were on the mountain so early," said Sergeant Lewis. He was middle-aged with a bit of a paunch and looked like he wished he was anywhere but here.

"I told you. I was going for a run."

"You're lying," said Dad. "You don't run. Not with that leg."

"I do so! You don't know anything, so shut up."

Dad took a step forward, and Pop put a hand on his arm.

"The boy's been running. Mira told me that," said Pop.

I glared at Dad, daring him to say anything. He glared back.

"Okay, so you were out for a run. Who was the girl who was with you?" said Sergeant Lewis. I'd tried to keep Casey out of it, but the mom and dad must have mentioned she was with me when we came down the hill.

"Just someone I know. We train together."

"And her name?"

"Casey. I told them at the police station."

"Casey De Vries?"

I looked up at him. I'd never told them her last name. It threw me off guard. "Yeah, I guess so. I don't know."

"Is this her?" He held up a picture. Casey's smiling face, her hair pink like it was before Christmas. You could just see a bit of her scar at the edge of the picture.

I nodded. Where had they got that photo?

"Can you respond with yes or no, please?" said Sergeant Lewis. "Is this the girl you were running with on Huckleberry Hill?"

"Yeah, that's her," I said and looked away from the photo. There was a drop of dried ketchup on the table, and I scratched at it with my fingernail. I hadn't heard from Casey.

"Did she light the fire, Leon?" said Sergeant Lewis.

"No—"

He put his hand up to stop me. "Think really carefully, Leon, before you say anything. You're in a bad position here. You were seen coming off the mountain, only minutes after the fire started, with a packet of matches in your hand. It's a public park. People's lives were in danger. It doesn't look good."

I knew how bad it looked. I'd been thinking of nothing else. But how could I turn on Casey? I wasn't a snitch.

Pop came over to the table and pulled out a chair. "Just tell us the truth, Leon," he said. "We think we know what happened already. We just need you to confirm it. This girl, Casey. We've got evidence that links her to another fire as well."

I looked up at him. "You do?"

He nodded. "That warehouse that went up on New Year's Eve. Her cell phone was found on the scene."

"No, you're wrong." I shook my head vigorously. "It can't be hers. She jumped into a pool with it at a party and—"

Pop and Sergeant Lewis and Dad were all looking at me, their expressions telling me what I'd already figured out. She'd lied to me about her phone. I swallowed and looked away. I couldn't speak.

"Her fingerprints were found on that book of matches, along with yours," said Sergeant Lewis. "She lit the fire, didn't she?"

I clenched my teeth together. She'd lied to me. She'd lit fires before. In the very warehouse I'd seen her sneak into weeks before. Had she been planning it even then? Was that why she'd gone in there that day? To scope it out? And what about Huckleberry Hill? Had she taken me up there knowing what she was going to do? There'd been a number of arson fires over the past year. Was that her?

"Didn't she, Leon?" Sergeant Lewis's voice was insistent.

I stared at the ketchup, scowled at it like it was responsible for all this, and then gave one short nod.

"Can you speak up a bit, please?"

I lifted my head and looked him in the eye. "Yes. Casey started the fire."

Chapter Twenty-One

I was suspended from school, grounded indefinitely and had all my phone and computer privileges taken away. With one snap of my fingers, I'd successfully turned Dad from an indifferent parent into a Nazi drill sergeant.

I didn't really care. I felt like crap. I lay on my bed and replayed everything in my head over and over and over.

I was so angry. Angry at Casey for lying to me, for not telling me anything about herself. That she hated her life, that her stepfather was abusive, that she wasn't just Zane Bailey's ex-girlfriend but was part of his gang, a gang I now knew was responsible for all sorts of vandalism around town, including setting fires. Angry that she'd kept it all to herself.

And I was angry at myself. All our training runs, our conversations in the park, on the beach, at cafés and over Messenger, all the Snapchats. How had I not seen it? How could I have spent almost a year with someone and not known what she was, who she was and what she was capable of? I'd known she was in trouble these last few months. I'd seen how stressed out she was. Why hadn't I said anything? Why had I just stood by and watched it happen? Was I so involved in my own pathetic problems that I couldn't even ask her how she was doing? If I'd taken the time to listen, would things have been different?

I would never know. Because I hadn't done any of that. I'd kept whining to her about my own life and offered nothing in return. And as much as I couldn't forgive her for lying to me, I couldn't forgive myself for letting her.

A week passed, and then Mom came home. I didn't know if I was glad to see her or not. I'd talked to her on Skype, that being the one thing Dad would let me do on the computer, and I could see how worried and disappointed she was. It was a hundred times worse in person.

"I knew I shouldn't have gone away," she said for about the fiftieth time. She'd already filled the fridge and baked enough cookies and cakes to feed the whole graduating class. "I should never have left you alone."

"Mom, your being away had nothing to do with it," I said.

She put a plate of brownies down in front of me and a glass of milk. I hadn't drunk milk since I was ten.

"If I'd been here you never would have got mixed up with that girl," she said.

I shook my head and stuffed a brownie in my mouth. It wouldn't have made difference, I'd made a point of not telling anyone about her, not even Sam and Riley.

Somehow I had known that none of them would approve.

The front door slammed, and I stopped mid-chew. Dad stomped into the kitchen.

"They've found her," he said without even saying hello. "They're questioning her down at the station."

I swallowed the half-chewed lump of brownie in my mouth. It felt like a dog turd going down. Casey hadn't been seen since the morning of the fire. Hadn't been home, hadn't shown up at her school on Monday morning. I'd been worried, really worried. But, of course, without my phone I hadn't even been able to try to reach her.

"Where was she?"

"LA. Working a street corner off Hollywood Boulevard," said Dad. "I'm telling you, Leon, you sure know how to pick them."

"David," said Mom.

"That's all right, Mom," I said, pushing away from the table. "I know exactly what Dad thinks of me. We cleared that up a long time ago."

I went back into my room and closed the door. I was beginning to understand what Casey might have been feeling. I couldn't stand to be in the same room as Dad anymore. We hadn't spoken more than ten words to each other all week, and that was ten words too many as far as I was concerned. He'd made up his mind about Casey and about me, and he wasn't going to let anyone change his opinion.

Maybe leaving would be the best thing after all. Not right away, but once I graduated. I could get a job, find a little place for myself, maybe a room in a share house. It had to be better than living with Dad. Being in the house with him watching me, waiting for me to fail, was driving me nuts.

Of course, Casey had thought she'd be better off on her own too. And look where that had got her. On the streets of LA. Arrested for prostitution and now charged with arson. Despite how angry I was with her, the thought of her facing court and going to juvie made my chest constrict with panic. Juvie was for thugs like Zane Bailey, dropouts who'd been in and out of trouble since they were ten and were never going to make anything of themselves. Not Casey. Not the Casey I knew anyway. Funny, courageous, stubborn, straight-talking Casey. She would wither up and die in juvie. But what about the Casey I didn't know? The secretive, danger-loving, vengeful Casey I'd seen at the top of Huckleberry Hill? The Casey who loved Zane Bailey? Who took revenge on her stepfather by setting fires and risking people's lives? Wasn't juvie exactly where she belonged?

I groaned and buried my face in my pillow.

There was a tap on the door, and I raised my head. Dad stood in the doorway, my computer tucked under his arm.

"I'm really not in the mood right now, Dad," I said and flopped my head down again.

I heard the door close and thought he'd gone, but then the mattress shifted as he sat down next to me. I rolled onto my back and edged as far away from him as possible.

"I just had a phone call from Sergeant Lewis," he said. "Casey De Vries confessed to everything."

I lay very still, wondering what would come next. How he would figure out a way to blame me anyway.

"She said you had nothing to do with the fire, that you tried to put it out. Is that true?"

He looked over at me, and I nodded.

"Why didn't you say something?" he said, clearly frustrated.

"I told you I didn't do it. You didn't believe me."

He shook his head slowly. "No, I didn't, and I'm sorry about that. But you've got to admit the evidence was overwhelming."

I ground my teeth together and didn't say anything.

"You've got a right to be angry," he said. "I should've known that you wouldn't be involved in something like that."

I sat up and propped myself against the headboard. I didn't say anything, just glared at him. If he wanted to apologize, fine.

There was no way I was going to make it easy for him.

He shook his head again. "I should have trusted you."

"Yeah, you should have," I said.

He was quiet for a long time, and I thought maybe that was the end of it. Then he took a deep breath.

"Leon, I haven't handled things very well since your accident last year."

I waited, unsure where this was heading.

"I had such hopes for you, Leon," he said. "College, a good career, all the things I didn't have when I started out. I wanted things to be better for you. When you broke your leg and we knew you wouldn't be getting a scholarship, well..."

"What? Say it."

"I was so disappointed."

"Disappointed in me. I know. You've made that clear."

"No, disappointed *for* you."

I swore softly. "And you think I wasn't?"

"Of course you were, but it was like that Leon I'd imagined in my head was gone.

145

I didn't know what to do about it. I felt bad for you and guilty that I couldn't help you, that I didn't have the money to put you through college without the scholarship. Quite frankly, I was angry. Not at you, but at the whole situation, and it was easier to just push it out of the way and try to forget about it than deal with it."

"Or with me."

He shrugged helplessly. "Yeah."

His admission took me by surprise. He'd never talked like this before, and it was weird.

He looked over at me. "I checked out, and there's no excuse for it. I just want you to know it won't happen again."

"Okay," I said. I was afraid he might try to hug me or something. I kept my distance, but he just stood up and headed for the door.

"By the way," he said, turning back. "I'm glad to hear you're running again. You must have been training pretty hard. Huckleberry Hill's not an easy climb."

I suppressed a smile. I wasn't going to let him know how good it felt to hear him say that.

"Good luck with the race at Santa Cruz. We'll all be there cheering you on."

My gut twisted. "You know about that?"

"Yeah, Casey said you've been training for it for weeks."

I sat back again. "I don't think I'll be doing the race," I said. "That was Casey's thing."

I thought he'd get that disappointed look on his face again and lecture me about giving up. But all he said was "That's a shame. From what Mom tells me, it was your thing too. She said you ran every day in New York. Rain or shine."

I shrugged. "I guess."

"Think about it," said Dad. "And don't let someone else's actions change your mind. You do what's right for you."

He closed the door behind him. I was left wondering what had just happened.

Chapter Twenty-Two

My feet were itching to hit the pavement again. I set out the next morning and ran down to the recreation trail along the coast.

I'd thought a lot about what Dad had said. His admission that he hadn't handled the accident very well had got me thinking. Maybe I hadn't handled it very well either. Sure, it was a setback, a big one, but when did sitting around feeling sorry for yourself ever get you anywhere? And I'd been pretty horrible to Sam and Riley too. It wasn't their fault I couldn't do track anymore. I was a bit embarrassed by some of the things I'd said to them, especially to Sam. No wonder they were avoiding me.

I ran past the aquarium and the wharf and on toward the beach, my thoughts going in never-ending circles. I couldn't change the past. All I could do was move on. Finally I reached the sand and flopped down in a heap, totally spent. I hadn't solved anything, but I felt better.

As I waited for my bus home, I started thinking about Santa Cruz. Only the day before I'd been dead set against it. It didn't seem right without Casey, no matter what she'd done. But now I found the thought of competing just wouldn't go away. We'd trained for so long. Both of us. Did I really want to throw that away?

Mom, Dad, Nan and Pop were all in the kitchen when I got back. After so many months of arriving home to an empty house, hearing their voices startled me, like I'd opened the door to find intruders had broken in.

They looked up at me and fell silent when I walked in. Nan stared into her coffee cup like she'd dropped her dentures in there.

"What's going on?" I said.

"Nothing," said Pop. "We just came over for a coffee and a chat."

"Okay." I went over to the sink and filled a glass. I could feel their eyes on me.

"Have a nice run?" said Mom. Her voice cracked, and I turned around and stared at her.

"Yeah, I did," I said. "Would you guys like me to leave so you can keep talking about me?"

"We weren't—"

"Yeah, you were," I said. "That's okay. I get it. I'll leave you to it."

I headed for the door.

"We were talking about the half marathon at Santa Cruz," said Dad.

That stopped me. I turned around.

"You've worked so hard to get fit for the race, Leon," said Mom. "Don't let that girl ruin this for you too."

My fist clenched around the glass without me telling it to. "*That girl* is the only reason I even signed up for it," I said. "And she has a name, by the way. It's Casey, remember?"

"Now don't get your back up, Leon," said Pop. "Your mother has a right to be angry with her. She got you into a heap of trouble."

"Yeah? Well, she did a lot of good for me too," I said. I gestured with the glass, and water slopped out onto the floor. "I never would have considered running again if it wasn't for her. Everyone was tiptoeing around, not wanting to hurt my feelings. Afraid I would go off the deep end if they even mentioned my leg or track. Pretending that everything was normal, that I could go back to the way things were before the accident."

"Don't you think you're exaggerating a bit?" said Dad.

"No. I'm not exaggerating at all. She was the only one who treated me like a normal person. She didn't care about my leg or track or what I used to do. I was just Leon, the guy she met at physio. I didn't have to pretend to be anything else."

"You don't have to pretend around us," said Mom. "We know who you are."

I shook my head. "That's just it, Mom. Everyone has their expectations. Everyone wants me to be something. Something I'm just not anymore. Good or bad." I glanced at Dad when I said this. "Casey had no expectations. She took me as I was, and, believe me, I know I haven't been the easiest person to be around this year."

"You've had a lot to deal with," said Nan. "Anyone would have been a bit cranky."

"Well, Casey's had a lot to deal with too, a lot more than me," I said. "She's been through some pretty crappy stuff. And while she may have done some stupid things, she's not a bad person. So cut her some slack, okay?"

I didn't wait for an answer. I went into my room and closed the door, resisting the urge to slam it. I was still holding the glass of water, and I put it down on the dresser before running my hands through my hair. I was surprised at how mad I was at them. Mad on Casey's behalf. I hadn't intended to defend her like that—it had just come out. A gut reaction.

Maybe gut reactions weren't such a bad thing. I'd been thinking so long about everything, and all it had done was make my head hurt. School, graduation, college, running. I'd been trying to reason it all out logically, and I was no closer to making a decision than I'd been at the beginning of the year. Maybe it was time to go with the feeling in my gut.

I lay on my bed, put my headphones on and cranked up Bon Jovi. The beat pounded in my ears, drowning out any sound from the rest of the house.

I would start with the race at Santa Cruz. My gut was telling me to do it. So I would.

Chapter Twenty-Three

Race day dawned bright and sunny. It was only April, but it was going to be a hot one. We arrived about an hour before the race was due to start. There was the familiar feel of nervous anticipation in the air. I fastened my race bib onto my shirt and started doing some stretching.

Dad was walking circles around me, staying loose. It was still strained between us, but I could tell he was trying. When he'd offered to run with me, I'd reluctantly agreed. I didn't want to put a damper on his newfound goodwill. Now, with the crowd milling about, the loudspeaker blaring instructions, and people talking and laughing, I was glad he was there.

"Okay, you know where the start line is, right?" said Dad.

"It's a bit hard to miss," I said, pointing down the gigantic blow-up gate on the corner.

"Great. Remember, you don't have to bust through the line straightaway. Everyone is timed electronically."

"I know that, Dad," I said. "We talked this through yesterday."

"Right." He looked a little nervous, his gaze darting around the place. Then he slapped me on the back. "Good luck then," he said and walked away.

"What the...?"

I'd started to go after him when someone grabbed my shirt and pulled me back.

"Whoa. Where do you think you're going?"

I turned to find Sam and Riley standing behind me, along with Charlie Bowen and

Andres Silva, a couple of juniors who'd been on the track team with us the previous year.

I was stunned.

"What's wrong, Leon? Aren't you glad to see us?" said Riley.

"Yeah, of course I am. What are you doing here?" I spluttered.

"Your dad called me," said Sam. "He thought you could use some running buddies."

"You guys are doing the race?" I said.

Sam gestured to the racing bib he was wearing. "These aren't a fashion statement, dude."

"Wow. I mean, that's great," I said, grinning. It was like old times, all of us running together. I looked around for Dad, but he was nowhere in sight.

"Why didn't you tell us you'd been training?" said Riley.

"Yeah, we could use you on the team," said Charlie.

I shrugged. "It's just jogging. Not real training like you guys do."

The loudspeaker called the runners for the half marathon to the start gate. We watched them crowd in, a few jostling for position at the front. A few minutes later the countdown started, and then they were off. The 10K crowd was next.

"You guys don't have to stick with me," I said as the leaders disappeared around the corner. The nerves were starting to kick in again, and I was getting twitchy. "I'm not very fast."

"After 10K no one's going to be very fast," said Sam.

"I'm just saying. I don't want to slow you down or anything."

"We get it," said Riley. "Come on. I don't want to be stuck at the back with the moms and their strollers."

We found a position somewhere in the middle of the pack. My stomach was turning over. Pre-race jitters. I got them at every meet. This couldn't be more different than running a sprint though. No individual lanes, no starting blocks, no grandstand of spectators, just a lot of sweaty bodies packed together, poised to move. It was positively claustrophobic. My gut twisted, and I blew out some air, hoping I wouldn't spew.

The countdown began and the pack started to move, like a slow-moving line of traffic. The serious competitors at the front went first, taking off at a healthy pace, and then gradually the others followed.

Charlie and Andres took off fast, darting past an older couple who looked like they'd been running together for fifty years. I kept up with them, Sam and Riley on my heels, until we got to the top of Beach Street Hill. They'd gone out faster than I liked, probably faster than I'd run since the accident, and I knew I couldn't keep up that pace. Not for 10K. We reached the cliffs and the road leveled out, the ocean below us on our left. I could hear the waves breaking on the beach, gulls squawking overhead. The air was thick with salt and seaweed. I dropped back a notch, let Charlie and Andres pull ahead and settled into a rhythm.

Sam and Riley stayed with me, matching their strides to mine. We loped along, three abreast, the sun warm on our faces, a slight breeze coming off the ocean. It felt good. It felt right. My head was clear, my mind thinking of nothing but the sensation of my feet hitting the pavement, my breath going in and out, my arms pumping in sync with my legs. I was in the zone, and the only thing that mattered was that I keep going, keep putting one foot in front of the other.

I took some water at the first station, barely breaking stride as I scooped up the cup. I gulped down a couple of mouthfuls and threw it away casually, like I saw everyone ahead of me doing. Near the turnaround point I spotted Charlie and Andres. They were chugging along, but they looked done in, barely holding a slow jog. People were passing them left and right.

I picked the pace up a bit as we swept through the turnaround and breezed on past them.

"See you at the finish line, boys," said Riley with a wave.

We were past the halfway point now, heading down the path along the cliff. I was beginning to feel it. My thighs were hurting, and my breathing was coming a little harder. This was where I'd always kept my eyes on Casey's back to stop myself from giving up, promising myself that I wouldn't stop until I'd caught up to her. Now there was no Casey ahead, just a bunch of strangers poking along at different speeds.

Ten kilometers was farther than I'd ever run before. Casey and I had planned on increasing the distance of our training runs in the last couple of weeks, had mapped out a few longer routes. Of course, those plans had burned to ashes along with the scrub at Huckleberry Hill.

I picked out a runner ahead of me, a young guy with a shaved head, wearing a bright yellow singlet and blue shorts. We were gaining on him, but slowly. I focused on his back, concentrated on closing the distance between us, shut out the pain and made myself keep going.

Riley and Sam were puffing and panting beside me. Riley had lost his rhythm. He kept slipping behind, then sprinting to catch up again. Until he stopped catching up. Then it was just me and Sam and the guy in the yellow singlet. Everyone else was invisible.

We ran past the second water station and then we were on the home stretch. Yellow Shirt was only ten or so yards in front. I looked to find a new target and spotted the beach up ahead. The finish line was down there somewhere, just waiting for me.

There's something about spotting a finish line that spurs me on. I caught sight of that beach and all I wanted to do was get there as fast as possible. Sure, I was hurting. My legs were on fire by this point, and heavy as lead, but it didn't matter. I lengthened my stride and kept my eyes on the water. Sam dropped back behind me, and then I was past Yellow Shirt as well. I raced down the hill and turned the corner into the parking area. The finish line was ahead.

I knew I didn't have much left in me. I'd used up all my reserves and then some. But I tried for a final burst of speed, a sprint to the finish. And then my feet hit the sand.

My right leg gave way, my foot sank into the sand, and I stumbled forward, windmilling my arms like a clown. Against the laws of gravity, I stayed on my feet, weaving sideways to regain my balance. I slowed right down and then jogged across the finish line. It wasn't the finish I'd imagined, the triumphant sprint to the end, arms raised in victory. But I'd done it. I'd finished—and in a decent time as well.

Chapter Twenty-Four

When it was all over, we headed to a beach-side café for brunch. Me, Mom, Dad, the guys and their parents, and Harvey Miller and his brother too. I hadn't realized that Harvey was in that group at the front. He had finished with the best time for boys nineteen and under. I wasn't surprised.

What did surprise me was that I came in third. I was pretty damn proud of myself. If someone had told me six months ago, or even a year ago, at the peak of my track career, that I'd be running a 10K race, let alone placing, I would have told them they were nuts. And yet here I was. And it was all because of a girl I'd met at physio.

It had been a month now since the fire at Huckleberry Hill. In all that time I hadn't heard a word from Casey. I didn't know if that meant she didn't want to talk to me or couldn't. A part of me knew I was better off without her in my life. She was a mess, mixed up in things far more serious than I'd ever imagined. But another part of me still yearned to hear her voice. To sit on the grass and chat about nothing, or laugh at a Snapchat she'd sent or hop on a bus, knowing she'd be waiting for me at the other end. I was still angry that she'd done what she had, that she'd lied to me, kept secrets from me. But I was also worried about what had happened to spur her to do those things. Worried about what was happening to her now, and what was ahead for her in the future.

As we walked back to the beach after brunch, I pulled Harvey Miller aside.

"Do you know a girl at your school named Casey De Vries?" I asked.

"Yeah, she was in my homeroom," he said.

"Was?" I said. "She's not anymore?"

"She dropped out about a month ago." He gave me a long look. "Why are you asking?"

"No particular reason," I said. "I just haven't heard from her in a while."

"Do you know her?"

"Yeah, sorta," I said.

Harvey shook his head. "Look, I'll be straight with you, Leon, 'cause you seem like a decent guy. And to be honest, I feel a bit guilty about what happened last year."

"Don't," I said. "It wasn't your fault. It was an accident."

"I know, but it's hard to forget." He shrugged. "Anyway, I don't know Casey very well. She's a junior and not really the sort I hang out with, you know?"

I nodded. Not the sort I usually hung out with either.

"Rumor has it that she started the fire at Huckleberry Hill." He stared at me for

165

a moment. "And that she was with a guy from Gilburn when she did it."

I didn't say anything.

"It was right after the fire that she dropped out," Harvey continued. "At least, I assume she dropped out. She stopped showing up anyway. Someone told me she was arrested for arson."

"Any rumors about where she is now?" I said.

"Sure," said Harvey. "Lots. But what I heard was that her stepdad got the charges dropped and sent her off to an expensive boot camp for delinquent kids. You know, those military-style ones where they basically drill you into submission."

"Geez," I muttered. Casey would hate that.

Harvey shrugged. "I could be wrong, but it sounds like something he would do. You know who her stepdad is, don't you?"

"No."

"Robert Marshall."

I shrugged. The name meant nothing to me.

"Ever heard of Luxor Air?"

"Yeah, of course."

"Well, he owns it."

My eyes widened.

"You know the big mansion on Silverado Drive?"

I nodded.

"That's where they live."

I whistled appreciatively.

"Yeah, they're loaded. At least, he is."

I tried to fit Casey into that image. The mansion on the hill, the manicured lawns, the fancy car that came with its own driver. I couldn't do it.

"You want my advice, Leon?" said Harvey.

"Sure."

"Forget about her. She's one of those people who thrive on drama. She's a magnet for trouble. Don't let her drag you into it."

I grunted. Not an agreement or a disagreement. Just an acknowledgment.

If what he'd said was true, I wouldn't be hearing from Casey anytime soon. I didn't know much about those boot camps, but I was pretty sure the kids weren't allowed any contact from the outside, not even from family. It sucked. Big-time. But the alternative was worse. Boot camp might drive her crazy, but at least she had a chance of turning things around. Juvenile detention would have sealed her fate.

I still didn't know what to think about the whole thing. Or about her. I knew I wouldn't forget her. Ever. And if one day a message popped up on my phone, or a Snapchat or a text, I couldn't guarantee I wouldn't answer it. I didn't know if I would be able to resist the temptation.

In the meantime, I had things to do. Plans to make. I still wanted to go to college, and if a scholarship was out of the question, I'd just have to do it some other way. Take classes part-time, get a job, whatever it took. And I needed to go back to see Grandpa. Soon, while he still remembered me.

"Leon! Let's go." Dad waved me over. "I told you I had a shift this afternoon."

I climbed in and pulled the door closed. He was back to his normal self, and that I could live with. No more silence, no more complaining behind my back.

As we turned onto the freeway and headed back to Monterey, I switched on my phone to check my messages. My finger moved automatically to Casey's name, and our latest conversation popped up. Only it wasn't a conversation—it was just me messaging her and hoping she'd respond. There were five messages, the last one sent that morning, before we left for Santa Cruz. As much as I hated hearing she'd been dragged off to boot camp, it made me feel a bit better to know she wasn't just ignoring them. When she finally got her phone back, those messages would be waiting for her.

I pocketed the phone and looked out at the passing scenery. I had a feeling I hadn't heard the last from Casey De Vries. In fact, I was almost sure of it.

Acknowledgments

Research is a big part of any book, and this one is no exception. And while the availability of resources on the Internet has made research infinitely easier, there is no better source than an experienced individual. I'd like to thank Dr. Carolyn Bond for sharing her knowledge of sports injury and the treatment of broken bones and burns. I'd also like to thank Jaime Spreen for sharing her experiences competing in fun runs and half marathons. Of course, any errors in detail are mine. The novel is fictional, and while I have tried to portray places and events as accurately as possible where they correspond to the real world, they are, by necessity, interwoven with fictional places and events as they occur in the book.

Sonya Spreen Bates is the author of several books for children and young adults, including *Off the Rim* and *Topspin* in the Orca Sports series. She grew up in Victoria, British Columbia, and has spent many years working with children with communication disorders, often writing her own stories to use in therapy. She lives in Australia with her family. For more information, visit www.sonyaspreenbates.com.